The Lost Legion's Trail

DAMON NELSON

VIDPENGUIN PRODUCTIONS

CHAPTER 1

Echoes of the Past

T HE BOARDWALK GROANED AS Ethan Blake left the surveyor's office. His boot caught a warped plank, sending a large splinter through his sole. "Christ's bones," he muttered, shaking his foot as the doorbell's clang followed him into Main Street's chaos.

A whiskey barrel rolled past, chased by two red-faced Chinese merchants shouting in a mix of Cantonese and broken English. Ethan dodged sideways, colliding with a swaybacked mare chewing tobacco spit off the saloon steps. The smell of burnt beans and unwashed miners hit him like a fist - same godawful stench every Thursday when the new prospectors rolled into town.

"Blake!"

The shout cut through the din. A gnarled hand thrust a parcel wrapped in oilcloth and twine at his chest. Postman Greeley's tobacco-stained grin revealed three remaining teeth. "Came up on the last freight wagon," he wheezed, breath reeking of rotgut. "Marked *Hold For Surveyor* - figured that's you now."

Ethan's thumb found the sender's mark - a crude L branded into the wax seal. His pulse kicked up. "Who brought this in?"

"Wagon master said it rode shotgun all the way from Deer Lodge." Greeley leaned in, onion stink rolling off his patched coat. "Funny thing -

driver claimed this box was waiting at the station since... hell, '63 maybe?" The old man cackled, phlegm rattling in his chest. "Ain't every day a man gets mail from the grave."

The package burned against Ethan's ribs as he bulled through the crowd. A muleskinner's whip cracked near his ear. Some fool's rooster went airborne in a flurry of feathers and curses. He ducked under a swaying sign for Hartley's Dry Goods, sharp left at the blacksmith's glowing forge - straight into the meaty flank of Sheriff Cobb's new Belgian draft horse.

"Watch your boots, Blake!" The sheriff's drawl carried over the anvil chorus. "That hammerhead's got a taste for toes."

Ethan didn't break stride. The town's edge loomed where packed dirt surrendered to scrub pine. His lungs burned - half from altitude, half from the tightness in his chest. Ten years since the mining company buried Pa's empty coffin, and now this damn box shows up?

He spotted the bench wedged between two lodgepole pines, its slats green with moss. Same perch where Ma used to sketch the valley while he chased horned lizards through the grass. The memory hit him square between the ribs - her faded calico dress, charcoal smudges on fingertips, that quiet humming she did when the light caught the mountains just right.

The twine snapped like dried sinew when he yanked it. Oilcloth fell away to reveal leather bindings gone soft with age. Ethan's throat closed. He knew that stitching - same crosshatch pattern Ma used on his childhood saddlebags. The top journal's cover bore a single word burned into the hide: **Agnes**

Wind moaned through the pines. Somewhere behind him, a coach horn blared. Ethan didn't hear it. His thumb brushed a coffee stain on the first page's edge - Pa's eternal mark on anything paper. The ink beneath swam as his eyes focused on the opening line:

December 12th, 1862 - Took the contract despite James' protests. The Legion claims their silver vein plays out, but these assay numbers tell a different story. If I'm right about the tributary running north from Granite Peak...

Ethan's hands shook. He flipped pages filled with coordinates and hand-drawn maps, each entry tighter and more frantic. Halfway through, a folded broadsheet slid loose - *Helena Independent*, dated June '63. The headline screamed: *Disaster at Granite Mine - 30 Souls Lost!*

Bile rose in his throat. Pa's last letter had arrived the week before that explosion. Nothing about mines or silver. Just talk of building a proper house come spring.

Cold seeped through his trousers from the damp bench. Some part of him registered the distant clang of the smithy's hammer, the sawmill's relentless whine. But here, in this quiet pocket of pines, the only sound was the rasp of aged paper as he turned page after damning page.

***

The leather binding crackled like old bones under Ethan's fingers. He ran his thumb along the spine's ridge where Ma had sewn in extra thread after he'd dropped that first journal in the horse trough at twelve years old. Same uneven stitching, same faint lavender scent clinging to the pages despite decades buried in someone's attic. Or a grave.

"Christ Almighty." The curse slipped out as brittle newsprint fluttered to his boots. That smudged broadsheet headline glared up from the dirt - *Disaster at Granite Mine* - and suddenly he was nine again, watching Ma slam her fist on the sheriff's desk hard enough to rattle the inkwell. *My husband didn't run*, she'd snarled, voice raw as fresh-stripped timber. *You find him.*

Ethan's boot heel ground the newspaper into mud. He flipped faster now, pages whispering secrets in that hybrid cipher only the Blakes could read - half surveyor's shorthand, half Ma's musical notation from her conservatory days. Coordinates danced with bass clefs. Mineral samples crossed staves.

"November '62..." His murmur tangled with the distant clang of the smithy's hammer. Pa's cramped handwriting spidered across the page: *Lode richer than reported. Told Foreman Carter estimates flawed. Insisted on second survey.*

Ethan's gut twisted. Carter's name stared back from three subsequent entries, each entry's letters angrier. Last one ended mid-sentence, inkblot exploding across the page like a bullet hole. He didn't need to check dates to know - that final splatter marked the week before Pa's last letter arrived. The cheerful one about building a porch swing.

Somewhere behind him, a mule team protested their load. Ethan barely registered the driver's Cantonese curses. His finger traced a margin sketch - crude but unmistakable. Three peaks. Two crossed pickaxes. The Blake family brand burned into yearling hides every spring.

"Granite range," he breathed. The map in his head superimposed modern claims over Pa's faded lines. If this sketch showed the true vein...

A gunshot crack of splitting lumber jerked his head up. Sawmill crew swarmed like ants across fresh-cut pine. Normal. Safe. Mundane. Ethan stared at them without seeing, the journal's vellum page crinkling in his whitened grip. Pa's coordinates didn't match the official mine maps. Not by half a mile.

He fumbled for his breast pocket, brass compass tumbling into palm. The needle spun wildly before settling northwest. Always northwest these days. Ethan pressed the cold metal against his temple, feeling the engraved B under his calluses. Pa's hand had carved that letter the day the fever nearly took him at twelve. *True north finds true men,* he'd rasped between coughs.

Wind ripped through the pines, showering needles over a spread journal page. Ethan froze. There, between soil acidity calculations and a grocery list, Ma's elegant script spiraled: *J. returned last night. More miners asking about the Legion. Told them same as always - stories for fools. But his coat...*

The compass slipped. Ethan caught it mid-air, brass edge biting flesh. Blood welled as he squinted at the smeared entry. J for James? Uncle James had died two winters back, took his war stories to the grave. What coat? What—

Hoofbeats thundered past, spattering mud across the journals. Ethan swore, shielding pages with his body. The rider whooped, drunk already though the sun hadn't cleared noon. Normal. Safe. Deadly dull.

"To hell with this." Ethan snapped the journals shut. Strings of saliva connected covers until he ripped them apart. The topmost journal fell open again, stubborn as a whorehouse door. His bloodied thumb left rust-colored prints on a sketched map - Pa's crooked star marking some nameless canyon. Same star he'd drawn on Ethan's slate lessons. Same star etched into Ma's headstone.

The compass needle quivered. Northwest. Always goddamn northwest. Ethan jammed the instrument against the map, brass edge aligning with penciled ridges. Needle tip kissed the canyon star. A dry laugh escaped him. Fancy that - true north finding true madness.

He stood abruptly, journal pages flapping like wounded birds. The sawmill's scream cut off mid-whine. Teamsters froze, whiskey bottles halfway to lips. Ethan blinked. When had the street emptied? Even the ever-present magpies had gone silent.

Slowly, he turned. Shadows stretched wrong somehow - pine boughs bending east when the wind blew west. His compass spun lazy circles. Somewhere beyond the livery, glass shattered. A dog's howl climbed octaves until it became something that raised neck hairs.

Ethan stuffed journals into his coat, fingers trembling. The compass bounced against his sternum as he moved, a frantic heartbeat against brass. First rule Ma taught him - when the land speaks, stop talking. Second rule - run if it whispers.

He took five steps before freezing. There, between the assay office and Chinese laundry, a shape flickered. Not quite man, not quite mist. The compass burned cold against his palm. Ethan's boot heels dug into mud as the shape dissolved, leaving only the acid tang of struck matches.

"Real subtle," he muttered to whatever watched from the aspens. The journals pressed against his ribs like armor plates. Northwest. Starred canyon. Legion's grave. Answers.

The compass steadied as he walked. Behind him, unseen things chuckled in the pines.

***

The brass compass bit into Ethan's palm as twilight settled its teeth into Whiterock. He blinked crusted eyes—when had the streetlamps flickered to life? His right boot had gone numb from pressing against the journal-stuffed satchel. The bench slats creaked as he shifted, leather coat stiffening in the cooling air like dried rawhide.

Three cowhands stumbled from the Silver Slipper, harmonizing a drunken ode to some Denver whore. Their boot heels cracked ice puddles in the rutted street. Ethan's breath plumed ahead of him, each exhale dissolving the last traces of his mother's spidery handwriting still burning behind his eyelids. Legion routes. Starvation winter. Blood price.

He was reaching for his tobacco pouch when the aspens across the street shivered wrong. Not wind-driven—a single convulsion rippling up twelve trunks in perfect unison. Ethan froze, thumb hooked in his vest pocket. The compass beneath his shirt throbbed once, cold as a gun barrel pressed to skin.

Then the mountains began to bleed light.

Ethan's head snapped west. Above the jagged peaks, the sky tore open in luminous gashes—violet slashes fading to corpse-green smears. The Valley's Breath pulsed like a living thing, tendrils licking downward to caress pine slopes. Somewhere behind him, a crate smashed. Horses screamed in their stalls.

"Christ alive," Ethan muttered around the sudden copper taste in his mouth. The journals seemed to squirm against his thigh. He remembered Ma's stories—how the Breath supposedly danced on massacre anniversaries, how trappers swore it sang in dead languages. His left hand found the compass through wool and cotton, the embossed "W" worn nearly smooth from a decade of worrying at it.

The lightshow intensified, emerald ribbons now twisting into shapes that made Ethan's eyes water. A half-remembered journal entry floated up —*If the valley breathes west, keep to shale. If it sighs north, trust nothing that bleeds.* Problem was, the goddamn thing was doing both at once.

A gunshot cracked northeast. Then another. Someone started bellowing in Mandarin. The town's stray dogs set up a chorus of yips that climbed into unearthly wails. Ethan shoved off the bench, knees popping like rifle reports. The satchel slapped his hipbone as he turned full circle, taking inventory—shuttered windows, bolted doors, one idiot kid peering from the livery loft before getting yanked backward by his collar.

The compass burned colder. Ethan fished it out, brass lid snapping open with a click that echoed louder than it should've. The needle quivered between NW and NNW, jerking like a dowser's rod over poisoned water. He squinted past the false aurora, toward the blacker mass where Granite Peak shouldered against lesser mountains. Starred Canyon lay that direction if Hartley's drunk cartographer could be trusted.

Another gunshot. Closer now. Ethan spat into the frozen mud. "Alright, you theatrical sonofabitch. I'm moving." He jammed the compass into his breast pocket where it could sear a reminder into his flesh, hefted the satchel higher, and took his first steps northwest. The Breath flared brighter in his periphery—approval or warning, take your pick.

By the time he reached the edge of town, the lights were dying. But the compass kept its new heading steady as a hanged man's stare. Ethan didn't glance back at the dark huddle of Whiterock. Didn't need to. The journals' weight and the cold brand over his heart were invitation enough.

CHAPTER 2

A Botanist's Quest

T
HE STEEL BEAST BELCHED smoke as it rolled to a stop, scattering chickens and children along Whiterock's main thoroughfare. Lily Chen stepped down onto the platform, boot heels punching divots in dirt packed harder than Shanghai cobblestones. Her fingers found the jade pendant before her lungs finished coughing up locomotive grit—three quick taps against carved herbs worn smooth by generations of healer's hands.

"Out the way, girl." A bull of a man in union stripes shoved past, crate of pickaxes balanced on his shoulder. Lily sidestepped into a puddle of mule piss, nostrils flaring at the ammonia sting. The town sprawled before her like a drunk's game of mahjong—clapboard buildings slapped together at conflicting angles, signs swinging in Cherokee syllabary and Cantonese beside faded English lettering.

She cut through the chaos, cataloging resources: apothecary's mortar-and-pestle flag, butcher's icehouse dripping red onto sawdust, blacksmith tongs glowing orange as hell's own chopsticks. Her thumbnail worried the notebook spine in her coat pocket. Five weeks Simon had left, maybe six if the fever broke clean.

The Gold Pan Saloon announced itself with piano keys mangling "Camptown Races" and a whiskey barrel rolling downhill to crush a terrier's paw. Lily ducked under the swinging doors, immediately regretting the lavender sachet she'd tucked in her bodice that morning—now clashing with sweat-stale wool and tobacco juice.

"Whiskey neat," she told the barkeep, sliding a nickel across wood sticky enough to trap flies. The glass he produced had last been cleaned during Polk's administration. She carried it toward a corner table, stepping over a passed-out miner snoring into his own beard.

Notebook open, pencil flying. *Pinus ponderosa* needles in clusters of three—good for poultices. *Arnica cordifolia* near the rail tracks, bruised petals suggesting overharvesting. Her free hand dipped into her skirt pocket, thumb rolling dried yarrow leaves into powder out of habit. The pendant swung forward, tapping paper as she leaned over her work.

"...like goddamn emeralds growing straight out the ground," slurred a voice two stools down.

Lily's pencil froze mid-stem.

The speaker wore enough animal pelts to constitute a felony against nature. His companion had a face like a half-healed burn—all scar tissue and one milky eye. They hunched over their drinks like vultures on a fence line.

"Told you Crazy Bill weren't lying." Scarface swirled his bourbon, watching amber liquid cling to glass. "That valley's got plants ain't in no White Man's book."

Lily's boot nudged her medical satchel under the table. The linen-wrapped journal inside—the one with her great-grandmother's precise brushstrokes detailing *xiǎo xīn cǎo*, the Heart's Ease herb thought extinct since the Ming Dynasty.

Pelts slammed his mug. "Fuck's a plant worth dying over?"

Scarface leaned closer, stringy hair brushing rim of his partner's ear. "You ever seen a Comanchero waste lead on guarding flowers?"

Her pencil resumed moving, capturing their reflections in the mirrored backbar—twisted mouths and darting eyes. The barkeep polished glasses with a rag blacker than his fingernails. Three cowpokes at the far end argued over a marked deck. Normal Tuesday shit.

"Place is warded." Scarface made the sign of the cross upside down. "Old magic. Rock formations like...like dragon teeth."

Lily's pendant warmed against her collarbone.

"Dragons my left nut. You're drunker'n Custer's ghost."

"Ask the Shoshone! They call it *Valley Where Shadows Grow*. Lost three trappers last fall—found 'em grinning like fools with bellies full of..."

The piano chose that moment to screech into silence. Every head turned toward the batwing doors where some fool had let sunlight in.

Lily snapped her notebook shut. Ice-blue eyes met hers across the room—miner's daughter by the roulette wheel, fingers frozen mid-spin. Recognition flickered. Not of Lily's face, but her type. The kind who asked questions.

"Another round, Charlie!" Pelts bellowed, slinging an arm around his companion. "We ain't paid to be sober."

Lily palmed her specimen jars and slipped out the back door where the alley reeked of hops and poor decisions. Her fingers trembled as they sketched dragon teeth in the margin of her notes. Simon's laugh echoed in memory—twenty years old and teaching her chess strategies between coughs. *"Always think three moves ahead, jiějie."*

A shadow fell across her page. The miner's daughter stood hipshot in the alley mouth, calico dress straining over a Colt Peacemaker. "Heard tell you're buying strange plants."

Lily didn't look up. "Depends what's strangling them."

"Rumor says the Chen sister from San Francisco pays silver for weeds."

"Rumors'll get your tongue cut off in some territories."

The woman spat tobacco juice an inch from Lily's boot. "Five miles north. Look for the lightning-struck pine."

"Any particular reason?"

"Let's call it professional courtesy between women trading in dangerous greens." She melted back into the crowd, leaving Lily staring at the tobacco splatter slowly dissolving varnish from her heel.

Somewhere behind the general store, a mule braved its fifteenth reproductive insult of the afternoon. Lily adjusted her pendant, tasting iron where she'd bitten her cheek. Valley Where Shadows Grow. Heart's Ease needed darkness to bloom—her great-grandmother's journal mentioned caves, bioluminescent fungi...

She recorked the yarrow powder. Time to see if Crazy Bill's ghost stories held better medicine than McGinty's Pharmacy.

***

The miner's daughter left tobacco juice eating through Lily's boot varnish and half a decent clue. Lily scooped mud from the boardwalk to neutralize the acid, fingers working automatic while her mind chewed on *lightning-struck pine*. Her great-uncle's journals mentioned electromagnetic properties in fulgurites—maybe Heart's Ease thrived near mineralized sand fused by...

Saloon doors slapped behind her. Two mule skinners at the bar hunched over whiskey chasers, their knuckles tattooed with old frostbite. "...valley where shadows grow taller'n men," the bearded one grunted. "Found a spring there bubbled black as patent ink."

Lily's pendant warmed against her collarbone. She slid into the nearest shadow, notebook already open.

"Bullshit," snorted the younger man. "Any water's clear up Sentinel way."

"Clear?" Bearded knocked back his drink. "Drank from that spring 'fore dawn. Woke midday with my pocketwatch rusted shut and three days missing." He tapped the brass timepiece at his belt, verdigris blooming across its face. "Sundial plants growing 'round there too— flowers open when your shadow touches 'em, not no sun."

Lilex root. Nightshade cousin. Simon's last fever dream had described petals unfolding like skeletal hands. Lily's pencil flew across the page, capturing the man's description of bioluminescent moss patterns that matched constellation charts.

A chair scraped to her left. "You're either the worst spy or best botanist in Montana."

The voice carried East Coast vowels sanded down by frontier grit. Lily kept sketching the mule skinner's gesturing hands—thick fingers demonstrating how sundial plant stems spiraled counterclockwise. "Spies get shot. Botanists get samples."

Ethan Blake's laugh sounded like a saw blade catching on green wood —brief resistance before smooth motion. He placed a glass of something amber between her inkwell and specimen jars. "Not many note-takers survive McGinty's rotgut."

"Not many eastern dandies recognize *Aconitum noveboracense*." Lily nodded toward the wolfsbane pressed between ledger pages. "Though yours lacked the distinct leaf serrations when flowering."

"Mother preferred her poisons metaphorical." Ethan turned the notebook sideways, blue eyes tracking her annotations on geothermal microclimates. "You're mapping thermal vents through plant distribution."

"Someone's been hunting Ghost Walker's Dance formations." Lily didn't look up from shading a rendering of corroded pocketwatch gears. "Five expeditions vanished near geothermal hotspots last month."

Ethan's thumbnail traced her margin notes about magnetic anomalies. "Vanished...or found what they weren't seeking?"

The saloon's piano launched into a deranged rendition of "Camptown Races". A prospector stumbled into the wolfsbane jar, sending purple petals drifting across Lily's observations on sporulating fungi.

"Seeking's costly." She rescued the manuscript page, fingers brushing Ethan's map case. The leather bore Blake family symbols tooled beneath newer scars—a compass rose devoured by vines. "Your mother's journals mention heartwood compasses?"

Ethan stilled. "They mention Chen family healers purging mercury sickness from silver miners."

A bottle shattered near the poker tables. Two drovers squared off over disputed aces, spurs chiming like ill-tuned church bells. Lily pocketed her pencil. "Heartwood compasses only point where the land allows."

"Whereas jade..." Ethan nodded at her pendant, now emitting faint chartreuse phosphorescence. "...responds to living currents."

Their shared glance lasted three heartbeats—long enough for Lily to note the healed burn scar peeking above Ethan's collar, old enough to have blistered during the Great Fire of '78.

"Y'ALL CHEATIN' BASTARDS!"

The drover's fist connected with a jawbone crack that cut through cigar smoke and piano discord. Chairs became missiles. A whisky barrel rolled into the fray, spraying cheap bourbon across Lily's notes.

Ethan flipped the table as a body crashed where his head had been. "Still think spies get shot faster than botanists?"

Lily ducked a flying spittoon, salvaging her wolfsbane jar. "Depends who's—"

A Bowie knife thunked into the wallboards beside her ear, vibrating an inch from the dried monkshood sample. Ethan yanked the blade free, testing its balance. "Copper handle. Custom smithing."

"Focus, Blake."

"Always." He sliced through a careening suspender strap, toppling an attacker into a whiskey keg. "That miner's directions mentioned cougar tracks north of—"

Lily vaulted over the bar, snatching a bottle of pure-grain alcohol. "Lightning kills more idiots than cats." She smashed the liquor across an advancing brute's boots, striking a match on her boot heel. "Run or roast."

The fireball illuminated Ethan's grin—all teeth and impending trouble. They hit the back alley as the saloon's front windows blew out in an alcoholic supernova. Somewhere behind them, Sheriff Hart started hollering about property damage.

Lily adjusted her pendant, now cool against her skin. Ethan examined his liberated knife under moonlight. "Copper's conductive."

"So's stupidity." She flicked charred notebook pages from her sleeve. "Meet at the livery. Dawn."

"Bring a lightning rod."

"Bring a better map."

He melted into the smoke-choked dark, footsteps echoing off the bank's iron vault door. Lily counted thirteen seconds before McGinty started howling about his ruined stock. Perfect. Exactly enough time to reach the telegraph office and encrypt a message to Simon's caretaker: *Found catalyst. Mercury antidote possible. Burn this.*

The night smelled of scorched rye and possibility. Somewhere beyond the rail yard, thunder rumbled across Sentinel Peak. Lily licked bourbon from her knuckles and plotted tomorrow's path—three moves ahead, little brother. Always three.

CHAPTER 3

Paths Converge

T HE SALOON'S TINNY PIANO dueled with a miner's off-key rendition of *Clementine* near the back, while a cloud of Virginia Brightleaf smoke hovered permanent-like above the card tables. Ethan Blake's bootheel kept time against the floorboards with the mechanical rhythm of a railroad spike driver, his left thumb working circles across the cracked leather of his father's compass. The journal pages smelled faintly of bergamot oil and gunpowder - Ma's perfume mixed with whatever shit Pa had been handling that last week before disappearing.

"Rainbow obsidian deposits... seven days ride northwest of..." Ethan's pencil stub hovered over his mother's looping script. His coffee had gone cold three annotations ago.

A shadow cut through the tobacco haze.

The woman didn't ask permission - just pulled out the chair opposite him like she owned every splinter in it. Her fingers brushed the journal's edge, calluses catching on rag paper. "You're following the Legion's trail." Not a question. The way she said it made his shoulder blades itch - like she'd caught him skinny-dipping in the Clark Fork.

Ethan leaned back, letting his coat fall open enough to show the Walker Colt riding his hip. "Depends who's asking."

She flicked her braid over one shoulder with a practiced jerk of her chin. The jade pendant at her throat caught the coal oil light, throwing green specks across the whiskey stains on the table. "Chen. Lily Chen. You mentioned needing a botanist in the Herald."

He'd placed a three-line ad. Three weeks ago. This woman had either been combing every backissue in the territory or someone talked. Ethan's thumb found the compass again, brass ridges biting flesh. "What's a proper horticulturist want with buried legionnaire gold?"

Lily's laugh came out sharper than a skinning knife. "Your flyer said nothing about treasure. Just some fool notion about..." Her fingers danced over the open journal page, tracing his mother's sketch of a crescent-shaped leaf. "...finding answers in the Whispering Peaks."

Ethan slammed the journal shut hard enough to startle the drunk snoring two tables over. The compass dug into his palm. "You ever seen fireweed choke out an entire hillside? Watched ghost orchids bloom where a man bled out?" He leaned forward, voice dropping to match the rumble of ore carts passing outside. "There's patterns in what grows where. Patterns that don't square with any goddamn survey maps."

Her fingers tightened around the chair's splintered backrest. "You're tracking mineral trails through flora distribution."

"Someone is. Was." He flipped the journal open to a dog-eared page - his father's blocky handwriting crowding the margins around a pressed trillium specimen. "Twenty-three years back. My old man thought if he cataloged enough..."

"Wait." Lily's hand shot out, pinning the page. Her thumbnail tapped a smudged annotation. "'Shadowbloom sighting unconfirmed'... Where did he...?"

Ethan watched her pupils dilate. Bingo. "Southeast slopes. Same area the Legion's last dispatch mentioned before..." He let the sentence hang like a half-set trap.

The bottle blonde serving wench chose that moment to slam two whiskeys on the table. Lily didn't blink. "That flower hasn't been documented since..."

"Since the Blackfoot burned their cultivation fields in '58. Yeah." Ethan pushed one glass toward her. "But if anyone could find a surviving patch..."

Her knuckles went white around the jade pendant. Outside, the noon train whistle screamed through Silver Creek's canyon walls. Somewhere between the second and third clang of the crossing bell, Lily grabbed the whiskey and knocked it back like patent medicine.

"My brother needs that bloom's pollen." She set the empty glass down precise as a surgeon laying tools. "How many guns you bringing?"

Ethan spun the compass on its chain, watching the needle quiver toward the mountains. "Enough to make the shadows nervous."

Lily stood abrupt enough to send her chair screeching. "I'll need to inventory your medical supplies. And borrow a pack mule."

He was already relatching the journal. "We leave at first light."

"Tonight. Moon's waning gibbous - better for spotting night-bloomers." She was halfway to the door before adding over one shoulder: "And Blake? Your father's notes on soil acidity are horseshit."

The batwings swung shut behind her. Ethan drained the remaining whiskey, tasting copper and possibility. Outside, the Ghost Walker's Dance swirled knee-deep through the street - ground fog that clung like a jilted lover. He thumbed fresh cartridges into his Colt, the click-clack louder than the piano's final discordant plink.

* * *

The whiskey burned better going down than coming up. Declan "Deke" O'Sullivan nursed his third glass, calloused thumb tracing the bullet scar carved into the mahogany bar - Silver Creek's version of historical markers. Three tables over, the Blake kid's compass chain clicked against his mother's journals like a pocket watch counting down to trouble.

"Lost Legion," Deke muttered into his glass. The words tasted like old gunpowder and regret.

His reflection in the bar mirror showed a face that hadn't seen an honest razor in weeks. Behind him, the Chen woman was arguing logistics with Blake, her jade pendant catching lamplight like green lightning. Deke's knuckles whitened around his glass. Twenty years since Fort Benton. Fifteen since the Rangers stopped looking. Still felt like yesterday's whiskey souring his gut.

The saloon doors burst open on a gust of Ghost Walker's Dance. Fog tendrils curled across the floorboards like probing fingers as Clara Benson strode through, spurs singing off-key. She clocked the expedition huddle faster than a mustang scenting water.

"Blake!" Her voice cut through the cigarette haze. Heads turned. A poker player dropped his cards. "Heard you're short a wrangler."

Ethan didn't look up from his map. "Heard wrong."

Clara hooked a chair with her boot, spun it backwards, and straddled the seat. "Rode drag on the Helena cattle drive. Broke eighteen mustangs single-handed last spring." She tossed a coiled lariat onto the table, the knots intricate as spider silk. "Ask Big Nose Kate about my Dutch oven biscuits."

Lily arched an eyebrow at the rope work. "Can you distinguish Asclepias cryptoceras from A. hallii under moonlight?"

"Can you lasso a cougar mid-leap?" Clara shot back, grin sharp as skinning knife. "We'll play to our strengths."

Deke's glass hit the bar harder than intended. Four faces turned his way. The Chen woman's pendant swung lazy circles, casting emerald patterns across whiskey stains. He stood slowly, chair scraping like a coffin drawer.

"Declan O'Sullivan." The name tasted foreign without a "Wanted" prefix. "Tracker."

Blake's eyes narrowed. "Heard an O'Sullivan ran with the Burned Hills Gang."

"Same man tracked Jeremiah Cole through the Bitterroots." Deke kept his hands visible, scars catching the light. "Found the Dawson Pass shortcut."

The compass needle shivered as Blake leaned forward. "You know why they called it the Lost Legion?"

"Same reason sailors don't name ships 'Invincible.'" Deke's collar chafed where the noose should've bit. "Your daddy's maps skip the ice caves."

Clara snorted. "Ice caves? Try the Spirit Canyon switchbacks. Lost three mules there last fall." She slapped a battered journal on the table - Barker's Illustrated Atlas, pages bristling with pressed sagebrush. "Moon phases, water sources, Pawnee warning glyphs. Better than your government surveys."

Lily flipped to a page marked with antler tines. "These altitude notations..."

"Took barometer readings myself." Clara's grin turned feral. "Nearly took a header off Whisper Rock getting the 8,000-foot mark."

Blake's finger traced her sketched ridgeline. "That's two days saved." His eyes flicked to Deke. "Three if we avoid snowmelt traps."

"Four," Deke corrected, "if you want to outrun Langston's boys." He jerked his chin toward the window where hydraulic monitors screeched in the distance. "Word travels faster than dysentery in a cathouse."

Lily's pendant darkened to stormcloud jade. Clara cracked her knuckles, the sound echoing through sudden silence. Somewhere a beer stein shattered. The piano player launched into "Buffalo Gals" with desperate enthusiasm.

Blake spread his mother's journals beside Clara's atlas. "O'Sullivan scouts ahead. Miss Chen handles botanical threats. Benson..." He eyed her rope burns. "Keep us fed and vertical."

"What about the ice caves?" Deke asked.

"We burn that bridge when we come to it."

Clara whooped, slamming her fist on the table. Glassware rattled as she produced a flask from her boot. "To jumping blind!"

Lily declined with a surgeon's glare. Deke took a pull - genuine Kentucky fire, not the panther piss Silver Creek peddled. It scalded away the ghost of rope burns around his neck.

Outside, the Ghost Walker's Dance coiled tighter around the saloon. Somewhere beyond the fog, the Sentinel Range waited with patient cruelty. Blake reloaded his Colt with shells that gleamed like bad ideas.

"Move out in twenty," he ordered.

Clara was already at the door, braid swinging like a pendulum counting down to chaos. "Last one to the stables buys the first round in Hell!"

***

The whiskey in Henry Thompson's glass caught lamplight like liquid gold, but his attention wasn't on the drink. Across the saloon's smoke-hazed interior, Blake's ragtag crew spread maps across a whiskey-stained table. Thompson's calloused thumb traced the scar on his temple - an old habit when calculating risk versus reward.

"Five percent finder's fee," he muttered to himself, watching the Chinese botanist adjust her jade pendant. "Ten if they actually survive the ice caves." His boot tapped against the floorboards in time with the piano's jaunty rhythm, but his mind raced through ore distribution charts and mineral rights laws.

At the expedition table, Blake's voice cut through the saloon din. "O'Sullivan takes point at dawn - your nose for trouble's better than any bloodhound's." The former outlaw grunted approval, fingers brushing the knife at his belt.

"Miss Chen," Blake continued, "you'll inventory our supplies against the Harmonious Botanical Medicine protocols." Lily nodded, her pendant shifting to deep forest green as she began scribbling in a weathered notebook.

Clara Benson nearly upended her chair leaning forward. "What about the Three-Nations Tent rig? My pa taught me-"

"We'll use your hybrid design," Blake interrupted. "But we lash the supports my way past the timberline." Clara's triumphant grin faltered halfway, morphining into grudging respect.

Thompson rose, chair scraping loud enough to draw pistols from three nearby drinkers. He approached with hands visible, that polished chuckle ready in his throat. "Mr. Blake, is it? Word is you're short on geological expertise."

Blake didn't look up from the soil analysis charts. "We're set, Thompson."

"Are you now?" Henry leaned over the table, catching the sharp herbal scent of Lily's disapproval. "The Silver Creek Hydraulic boys missed a quartz vein right under their stamp mills last month. You think your mother's journals account for glacial sediment shifts?"

The compass in Blake's hand stilled. Clara cracked her knuckles loud enough to echo. Somewhere upstairs, bedsprings squeaked in rhythmic counterpoint to the mounting tension.

"Five percent contingent fee," Henry pressed. "I get you through the Sentinel Range fissures without losing a pack mule."

Lily's teacup clattered against its saucer. "Your mining operations poisoned seven square miles near Butte."

"And I've got the surveys to prove where *not* to dig." Henry's smile showed teeth. "Accidents happen faster than dysentery in the high country, Blake."

The journal pages rustled as Blake flipped to a map dotted with his mother's precise notations. "Two percent. And you walk point with O'Sullivan through the shale fields."

"Four and I'll share Langston's survey markers from '78."

"Three, and you don't mention Langston again." Blake's pencil snapped mid-sentence.

Henry raised his glass. "Welcome to payroll."

Deke spat a stream of tobacco juice that barely missed Henry's boot. "Fancy boy gets eaten first when the wendigo show up."

Clara produced a battered harmonica. "Anyone know 'Old Dan Tucker'? Proper send-off music."

As the others argued route priorities, Blake slipped his father's compass into his breast pocket. The metal felt heavier tonight - not with doubt, but the sharp certainty of poisoned streams and dynamite scars marring the Hidden Valley. Outside, the Ghost Walker's Dance swirled around a dead hitching post, whispering of bare branches that could pierce a man's palm like crucifixion nails.

"Moon's up," Blake announced, rolling the maps. "Saddle the hybrids. Benson - check those Three-Nations Tent poles again."

Clara mock-saluted with her harmonica. "Yes sir, boss sir."

Lily paused in the doorway, her medical kit clinking with tinctures. "The Living Terraces won't forgive intrusion lightly."

"Neither will I." Blake checked his Colt's cylinder - six shells gleaming like mercury tears. "Move quiet, shoot straight, and maybe we all come back rich."

Henry lingered as others filed out, eyeing the journals. "Your mother's notes on the shale formations-"

"Earn your three percent first." Blake's shadow loomed large against the peeling wallpaper. "That scar looks recent."

"Colorado silver strike gone wrong." Henry's grin didn't reach his eyes. "Makes a man... reevaluate partnerships."

The saloon doors swung shut behind them, cutting off the piano's drunken chorus. Somewhere in the Sentinel Range, a rockslide chuckled to itself. Blake adjusted his pack straps, the journals' weight a familiar anchor against his spine. Let the Ghost Walker's Dance try to swallow them whole - he'd carve directions in its misty flesh if needed.

Clara whooped as her horse reared. Lily murmured to her pendant. Deke lit a cigarillo with hands steadier than a hangman's rope. Henry Thompson checked his specimen bag with the intensity of a gambler counting cards.

Blake took point without looking back. The compass needle quivered north-by-northwest, toward ice caves that whispered his father's name.

CHAPTER 4

Whispers of the Land

T HE SMOKE FROM ELLIE Red Feather's campfire curled upward like a question mark. Ethan Blake waited three paces outside its light, hands loose at his sides – close enough to show intent, far enough to avoid presumption. His mother's journals pressed against his ribs beneath the oilskin duster, their secrets itching like unscrubbed gunpowder residue.

"You gonna stand there letting mosquitoes drink their fill," Ellie said without turning, "or you got actual business?"

Ethan tipped his hat brim lower to hide the grin tugging at his mouth. "Heard tell you know stories about these hills that don't end with 'and then the cavalry came.'" He palmed a twist of tobacco from his vest pocket, laid it on a flat rock near the fire's edge. "Care to share one?"

Ellie's braids swung like pendulum weights as she turned. Firelight caught the obsidian edges of her eyes. "Sit. Keep your damn trade goods. Stories ain't currency here."

He folded himself onto the damp earth, Winchester balanced across his knees. The fire popped, sending up a spray of sparks that tangled briefly with the stars before winking out. Ellie stirred the coals with a stick carved in spirals that hurt to look at too long.

"Your people talk about veins of silver," she began. "Mine speak of bloodlines older than mountains. When Thunder Being coughed up these peaks, his spit became rivers. His breath..." She snapped a dry twig, tossed the pieces into the flames. "That's what you white coats measure with your barometers and call 'weather patterns.'"

Ethan leaned forward, forearm resting on the rifle's receiver. "And when that breath gets restless?"

Ellie's smile showed teeth. "Depends. You ever seen snowflakes dance sideways in July? Heard whispers in aspen leaves when there's no wind?" Her stick jabbed westward where the Sentinel Range's silhouette ate the horizon. "Valley's Breath wakes when something stirs that oughta stay buried."

The fire dimmed sudden as a snuffed candle. Ethan's hand found the Colt at his hip before he registered the lack of heat. Cold moonlight revealed tendrils of mist coiling around their boots – ground-hugging fog that smelled of wet stone and something metallic.

"Well hell," Ethan muttered. His breath plumed white despite the August night.

Ellie didn't move. "Don't blink, Blake."

In the campfire's dying embers, orange streaks pulsed like liquid circuitry. The coals rearranged themselves – not in some haphazard glow, but forming deliberate lines that etched a topographic map in fire. A narrow pass here, sheer cliffs there, and dead center...

"Is that–"

"Shut up." Ellie's command carried the weight of glacier ice.

The spectral cartography sharpened. Ethan's pulse hammered against his collar as the burning lines resolved into a box canyon no wider than a rifle shot, its walls marked with symbols that matched the scars on nearby boulders they'd passed yesterday. The vision held for three heartbeats before collapsing into mundane ash.

Ellie spat into the darkness where the fire had been. "Ancestors just drew you a damn treasure map. Hope you're good at reading between the lines."

Ethan scooped a handful of still-warm ash, let it trickle through his fingers. "Any chance they'll send clearer directions next time? Maybe a guide who doesn't speak in riddles?"

The smirk Ellie shot him could've curdled milk. "You wanted old stories. Got 'em." She stood in one fluid motion, medicine pouch swaying at her belt. "Word of advice? When the land starts talking, even fools listen. Doesn't mean they understand."

He watched her melt into the pines, mist clinging to her braids like spectral fingers. The Colt's grip felt slick in his palm. Somewhere past the tree line, an owl screamed twice – not the soft hoots from storybooks, but the raw screech of something tearing meat from bone.

Ethan reloaded his Winchester by touch. "Directions could've included where the hell I'm supposed to sleep tonight," he told the empty clearing. The ash-streaked ground offered no reply.

***

Ellie's fingers brushed the beaded necklace at her collarbone, the gesture older than whiskey and twice as bitter. "That ravine you saw? Ancestors call it *hé ǧlá* - where shadows chew daylight." She kicked ash over the dead fire with a battered moccasin. "Go poking round there, you best bring more than bullets and arrogance."

Ethan watched a scarab beetle crawl across the soot-darkened stones where flames had danced minutes before. "Meaning?"

"Meaning don't pick fights with rocks that remember dinosaur farts." Ellie's laugh held edges sharper than her skinning knife. She tugged a braid loose, black hair spilling over buckskin shoulders. "Your people write warnings on paper. Ours carve 'em in bones."

He stood, Winchester stock worn smooth against his palm. "And if the bones lie?"

The medicine pouch at Ellie's belt rattled as she turned. "Then you'll make fine fertilizer for coyote weed." Her footsteps faded into juniper scrub, leaving behind the scent of crushed sage and unspoken threats.

***

Twenty yards east through scraggly pines, Lily Chen's mortar made rhythmic thunks that echoed rifle reports. Moonlight caught the glass vials spread across her bedroll - tinctures numbered in precise Mandarin characters, their stoppers crusted with red desert dust.

"Three parts yarrow," she muttered, squinting at leather-bound pages foxed with age. The jade pendant swung free as she leaned closer to her great-grandmother's spidered script. Its usual sea-green depths pulsed faintly, matching the tempo of crushed bluebell roots staining her fingertips.

A nightjar's cry splintered the dark. Lily's head snapped up, left hand already palming the derringer from her boot. The pendant's glow intensified as wind shifted through nearby sage - not the arid gusts that baked lips cracked, but something damp and murmurous.

"Not now," she told the heirloom, tucking it under her collar where cold stone met sternum. The glow dimmed reluctantly. Her field journal lay open to yesterday's entry: *Specimen 27-C: Possible antispasmodic properties. Test with caution.*

She measured five drops of mescal extract into the mortar, nostrils flaring at the acrid sting. The mixture fizzed purple. "Better." Her grandmother's tincture formula demanded precision - quarter-ounce variations had turned militia surgeons' hair white back in Shandong province.

Boots crunched pine needles behind her. Lily didn't turn. "If you're here to ask about sleep tonics again, Marshal, I need six rattlesnake tails first."

"Just admiring your dedication to poisoning yourself." Ethan's shadow fell across the mortar. "That the same brew that dissolved McCready's tin cup?"

"Different alkaloid profile." She adjusted the brass loupe strapped to her forehead. "This one dissolves hubris. Care to volunteer?"

His chuckle sounded tired. "Tempting." A folded map slid beside her vials. "Red Feather says there's a valley northeast that..."

"Eats daylight. Yes, I heard." Lily's pestle never paused. "Tell me when you find corpses missing their livers. That's usually chapter two in these stories."

Ethan's silence lasted three heartbeats. "You don't believe in-"

"I believe in liver-eating beetles. Also dehydration and fools who wander off cliffs reading poetry into rock formations." The pendant throbbed once, sharply, against her breastbone. She ignored it. "What I know is cardiac glycosides in desert lilies can stop a man's heart in ninety seconds. Priorities, Marshal."

When she finally looked up, only the map remained, corners weighted with .45 caliber shells. Somewhere beyond camp, the wind whispered through juniper branches like a woman humming forgotten words. Lily's mortar clicked twice as the last bluebell root surrendered its juice.

The pendant glowed again, fierce enough to silhouette her thumb bones through flesh. This time, she didn't smother it.

***

Ethan rolled the obsidian arrowhead between his fingers, the black stone drinking moonlight. Ellie's words clung like burrs—ancestor visions weren't part of the geological surveys he'd memorized. Across the dead firepit, the shaman woman waited as patient as canyon walls.

"Your people's stories..." He chose each word like stepping stones across a river. "They ever mention quartz veins running northeast? Iron deposits?"

Ellie's braids swayed as she shook her head. "Mountains remember footsteps, not ore. The valley you seek breathes when trespassers come." She nodded toward his map case. "Your lines on paper scream where they should whisper."

A gust funneled down from the Sentinel Range, carrying the metallic tang of distant rain. Ethan's survey notes fluttered against the .45 shells anchoring their corners. When he looked up, Ellie was gone—just juniper branches swaying where she'd stood moments before.

"Son of a..." He snatched his collapsing ruler before it tumbled into ashes, brass joints clicking. The arrowhead left crescent moons in his palm. Through gritted teeth: "Appreciate the guidance."

Somewhere in the darkness, leather creaked against rock. "The Breath favors fools who listen." Ellie's voice came from three directions at once. "Even pale ones with pretty eyes."

He thumbed the revolver's checkered grip on reflex. Twenty-eight years old and still jumped at parlor tricks. The camp's edge dissolved into shadow where starlight drowned in pines. His mother's journals suddenly felt heavier in the saddlebag.

***

Lily Chen spat cherry pits into the fire, each one hissing as it hit coals. "Diagnosis?" She didn't look up from grinding what looked like dried caterpillars in her mortar.

Hank coughed into a bandana already stiff with phlegm. "Like a mule kicked my ribs, doc."

"Bronchitis. Also stupidity." She tossed another branch on the flames. "Who strips naked to ford glacial streams in October?"

The cook reddened beneath his salt-and-pepper beard. "Said I was hot!"

"You're an idiot. Hold this." Lily shoved a clay cup against his chest. The liquid inside shimmered oil-slick green. "Drink it all before I decide you're Darwin's problem."

As Hank gagged, her jade pendant flared—three quick pulses like a dying man's heartbeat. She caught the stone mid-glow, fingertips finding the Chen family glyph carved on its back. The usual excuses lined up: static charge, reflected flames, tired eyes. Never mind that the damn thing had started humming during yesterday's landslide.

"Another round?" Hank wheezed, cup trembling in his hands.

"Pray you don't need it." She scraped resinous paste into a tin labeled **BOVINE LETHARGY / MAYBE TYPHOID**. The pendant's heat lingered like a brand between her breasts.

Across camp, Blake emerged from the dark holding his hat like a damn tea saucer. Moonlight caught the sweat line where his Stetson usually sat. Lily's mortar clanged as she dropped it.

"Your pet mystic vanish again?" She nodded toward his map clutched underarm. "Let me guess—we follow the weeping maiden's ghost at dawn?"

Blake's knuckles whitened on the map tube. "We're adjusting course to avoid rock slides."

"Rock slides." Lily pulled a hairpin from her bun, using it to dislodge bluebell pulp from the pestle's grooves. "Not vengeful spirits? Portents? Singing fucking coyotes?"

The marshal's boot sole scritched against granite. "You notice any tremors around midday? Soil displacement could—"

"Save your lies for the investors." She flicked gunk at his boots. "I need plant samples from the north ridge. Spirit attacks won't interfere, will they?"

His jaw muscle jumped. Proper Eastern gentleman playing frontier hero. The jade stone seared her skin when he stepped closer.

"You'll have guards," Blake said.

"I always do." She turned back to her poisons, mortar cracking like gunshots. "Tell your riflemen to watch their feet. Prairie nettles make men piss blood."

When she finally glanced up, Blake was just another shadow merging with the pines. The pendant cooled slowly, leaving her collarbones threaded with frost despite the fire. Lily added four drops of monkshood extract to Hank's next dose.

Rational thought required evidence. Controlled experiments. Data. Not some backwater mystic's ghost stories paired with a mineral's tantrums. She stirred the brew counterclockwise, chanting the Chen purification rhyme under her breath—strictly chemical reactions, nothing more. If the liquid turned clear instead of blood-red tonight, she'd blame altitude sickness.

Always a reason. Always an equation. The alternative made .45 caliber plans go sideways.

CHAPTER 5

The Journey Begins

THE HORSES STAMPED IMPATIENTLY at the edge of civilization, nostrils flaring plumes of vapor into air sharp enough to cut glass. Clara spit tobacco juice that froze before hitting the ground. "Either we move now or start building fucking igloos," she muttered, slinging her Sharps rifle across the saddle horn with practiced ease.

Deke wordlessly adjusted the straps on his pack, green eyes never stopping their restless sweep of the tree line. His Bowie knife caught the faint light when he turned – five inches of carbon steel that'd field-dressed more game than most men saw in a lifetime.

Ethan tightened the last buckle on his saddlebag, leather stiff under his gloved fingers. When he turned toward town, the lanterns still burning in Hartley's General Store winked like drunken fireflies. Somewhere behind those frosted windows sat the cracked leather journal that started this madness, its pages still smelling faintly of his mother's rosewater despite fifteen years in an attic trunk.

"Nostalgia's a luxury," Deke grunted, already moving upslope into the pines. "Bears don't give a shit about poetry."

Lily fell into step beside Ethan, her worn boots crushing frozen bracken. "Ignore him. My grandfather said ghosts walk easiest at daybreak." She pulled a sprig of something from her coat pocket – dried and twisted like old bones. "Sweetfern. Chew it when you need to stay sharp."

"That your answer for everything? Botanicals and dead relatives?"

Her teeth flashed white in the predawn gloom. "Worked through three plagues and my uncle's second wedding."

The trail narrowed as they climbed, Deke's broad back disappearing then reappearing between lodgepole pines. Frozen mud gave way to scree that skittered underfoot – nature's landmines waiting to twist an ankle. Ethan's mare snorted protest when he urged her up a shale-covered incline, hooves sliding on stone slick with ice.

"Easy girl," he murmured, leather reins cold against his palms. The compass in his breast pocket pressed against his ribs like a second heartbeat. Last thing his father ever touched before riding out for supplies that storm-choked November. Came back frostbit and coughing blood, mumbling about blue lights in the cedar swamp.

"Blake!" Deke's bark shattered the memory. The tracker stood statue-still ahead, gloved hand raised. Every muscle in his corded frame screamed tension. "Wolf sign. Fresh."

Clara swung down from her bay, brass cartridges jingling as she crouched beside the tracks. "Big bastard. Loping, not hunting." She rubbed snow between thumb and forefinger. "Two hours old. Moving east."

Lily crouched to examine trampled brush nearby. "Not wolves." She held up a mangled branch, sap oozing amber where teeth had scored deep grooves. "Moose. See the bark stripping?"

Deke's shoulders relaxed a fraction. "Could still draw predators."

"Could still win a poker game naked in hell," Clara snorted, remounting. "Either shoot something useful or quit pissing your britches."

The trail widened into a game path as morning bled gray through the pines. Lily kept pace alongside Ethan's horse, cataloging the forest like a walking field guide. "Yellowroot there – boil it for fever. Those serrated leaves? Poison sumac. Wipe your ass with that and you'll be shitting through a guitar string."

Ethan watched her finger brush a cluster of withered berries. "What's that one kill?"

"Nothing." She popped one in her mouth. "Wintergreen. Makes your breath smell less like a bear's asshole."

Somewhere ahead, Clara started humming "Camptown Races" off-key. Deke muttered what sounded like a prayer in gaelic. The compass warmed against Ethan's chest as they pushed deeper into country where maps ended and legend began.

The mules kicked up clods of frostbitten earth as Deke jerked his chin toward the northern tree line. "Sun's wasting." He spat a wad of tobacco that steamed where it landed. "Any slower and we'll be hunting our own ghosts for supper."

Ethan's gloved hand drifted to the compass beneath his coat. Through moth-eaten wool, he traced the embossed B – Blake, Benjamin, bullshit family legacy carved in brass. Whiterock's chimneys poked skeletal fingers above the pines behind them, smoke curling like question marks in the slate-gray dawn. Somewhere in those weathered clapboard buildings, answers moldered between church registry pages and saloon ledgers.

"Move or mourn, college boy." Clara's mare sidestepped, iron shoes sparking against flint. "Ain't getting any prettier back there."

They fell into formation behind Deke's sway-backed gelding – ex-lawman turned tracker three steps ahead of a lynch mob. Ethan noted how the man's shotgun never quite pointed groundward, the way his eyes catalogued snapped twigs and disturbed leaves like reading scripture.

Lily materialized at Ethan's elbow, pointing to a gnarled shrub clawing through the frozen mud. "Devil's club." She snapped off a thorned stem, amber sap bleeding over her knuckles. "Salish use it for arthritis."

"Also works great for stabbin' fuckers," Clara called over her shoulder.

The botanist's laugh hitched higher than her usual speech. "Boil the roots with stinging nettle..." Her boots crunched through ice-crusted puddles, words tumbling faster than the mountain streams cutting through limestone. "...add minced yarrow for hemorrhage control... elderflowers reduce inflammation..."

Ethan watched a red squirrel freeze mid-trunk as Lily rattled off anticoagulant properties. The compass felt heavier with every step. His father had carried this same brass weight through these woods, pockets full of cryptic notes and hands stained with ink instead of medicine.

Deke halted so abruptly Clara nearly rode up his ass. "Two-legged jackrabbits," he growled, crouching by Deke's callused thumb brushed fresh boot prints sunk deep in loam. "Two hours old," he muttered, voice like gravel under wagon wheels. "Carryin' iron."

Clara swung down from her paint mare, spurs chiming death knells against stone. "Bandits?" Her hand drifted toward the Colt Navy at her hip, fingers dancing the way they did when gentling skittish yearlings.

"Worse." Deke spat black tobacco juice that sizzled in the snow. "Fools."

They pushed harder after that. The forest closed around them like a fist - white spruce branches clawing at coats, frostbitten bracken snapping underfoot. Ethan's breath came in plumes that lingered too long, as if the cold itself weighed them down. Somewhere ahead, water chuckled dark promises.

Lily appeared beside him, jade pendant glowing dully against her scarf. "That's ghost pipe," she said, nodding to pallid stems thrusting through ice. "Grows where bears winter." Her mittened hand brushed his sleeve. "Your mother's journals mention these groves?"

"Not yet." The lie tasted like last week's beans. Page 83 of Margaret Blake's third journal showed this exact copse drawn in maddening detail, right down to the lightning-scarred cedar marking the game trail. His gut churned seeing it in flesh and sap.

Clara's laugh shattered the gloom ahead. "Y'all smell that?" She stood framed in dying light where the trees broke sudden and clean. Below them, Silverthread Creek gnawed at its icy banks, waters smoking in the dusk. "Digger pine resin," she called back, nostrils flaring. "Means hot coals hold all night."

They made camp with the grim efficiency of folks who knew darkness brought teeth. Deke paced the perimeter, shotgun cradled loose and lethal, while Clara tended the horses with quick hands that belied her chatter. Ethan watched Lily bundle fir needles into muslin squares - pneumonia poultices, she'd explained earlier, though her eyes kept flicking to his pack where the journals slept.

Fire bloomed violet from salt-cured wood. Shadows stretched long over tin plates of beans and venison. Ethan waited until Clara started cleaning her pistol - methodical strokes of oilcloth down the barrel - before spreading the journals across bedrolls.

"Christ on a crutch," Clara breathed. The firelight danced across Margaret Blake's spidery notations, illuminating fever-drawn maps where rivers ran backward and mountains crouched like waiting beasts. "Your ma drew these... before?"

"During." Ethan's finger found the cipher he'd broken at sixteen - three spirals meant DANGER, five crosshatched lines signaled FRESH WATER. "She spent three summers charting the Sentinel Range. These symbols..."

"Mark ambush sites." Deke's knife tip hovered over a cluster of inverted triangles near a sketched pass. "Blackfoot hunting grounds. Stumble in there with your pecker in the dirt..." The blade snapped shut.

Lily leaned close, jade pendant dangling over a margin crowded with herbological notes. "These glyphs match medicinal carvings at Fort McKenzie's apothecary." Her gloved finger traced overlapping circles. "This isn't cartography. It's recipe code."

Clara snorted. "For what? Witch stew?" But her hands stilled on the Colt's cylinder, one chamber empty where her pinky rested.

Ethan turned a page brittle as autumn leaves. "See these lunar phases paired with root sketches? She tracked harvest times. Belladonna here," he tapped September's waning moon, "ginseng here under snowfall." The compass in his pocket throbbed like a fresh bruise.

Deke stood abrupt, scattering shadow-wolves from the firelight's edge. "First watch." He vanished into the aspens without looking back, leaving his bedroll tight enough to bounce a nickel off.

Later, when the coals sighed ash and Clara's snores rasped like a sawmill blade, Lily whispered, "Your mother didn't just document plants." Her breath fogged the space between them. "She mapped power. The Valley's Breath thrums in these pages."

Somewhere in the dark, ice cracked like a rifle shot. Ethan said nothing, watching the jade pendant pulse soft as a fox's heartbeat against Lily's throat.

***

Deke spat a stream of tobacco juice that sizzled in the fire's embers. "You hear a twig snap that ain't from your own clumsy boots, you holler." He didn't wait for Ethan's nod before melting into the aspens, Winchester cradled like a lover. The man's shadow merged with the pines—just another predator stalking the dark.

Moonlight bled through the canopy as Deke paced the perimeter. Fourteen steps east. Pause. Listen to the creek's chatter. Twenty-three west. Halt. Track the screech owl's hunting cry. Routine kept a man alive. So did knowing when the woods went wrong.

The mist came quiet as a grave robber. One heartbeat the air smelled of pine resin and Clara's godawful snoring. The next, frost crept across Deke's beard. His knuckles whitened on the rifle stock. "The hell...?"

It slithered between trees—pale fingers snuffing out stars. The owl fell silent mid-hoot. Even the damn crickets quit their racket. Deke's boot sole crunched a frozen blade of grass. Too cold for September. Too still for living earth.

"Blake!" His bark sliced the silence. No answer but the mist curling around his ankles, thick as sheep's wool.

***

Ethan dreamed of his mother's hands. Ink-stained, gripping a pen as wind howled through Whiterock's shutters. *The ledger lies*, her voice rasped from the journal pages. *They'll come for the—*

A wet nose pressed his cheek.

He jolted upright, dislodging the coyote pup sniffing his bedroll. The creature vanished into swirling fog. Firelight barely pierced the haze cloaking camp. Ethan fumbled for his revolver.

Ssssst.

The sound skittered across his skull. Not heard—but felt, like a spider down his collar. He stood, blanket falling away. Cold bit through his union suit.

Boy.

Mom's voice.

Liar.

Pa's whiskey growl.

Ethan stepped toward the tree line. Compass iron seared his thigh through denim. "Metallic conduction," he muttered. "Frost forming on the..." The rationalizations crumbled with each step. Shapes writhed in the mist—a fractured parade of antlered shadows and hunched figures carrying lanterns that burned black.

Deke materialized beside him, rifle aimed at nothing. "You got a death wish, college boy?"

"Do you hear—"

"Hear what?" The tracker's eyes darted like cornered wolves'. "This ain't fog. It's the Valley's Breath. Swallowed two drovers whole last winter. Found their ponies a week later—still saddled, tongues blue as indigo."

The mist thickened. Ethan's compass vibrated against his leg. Somewhere beyond sight, hooves clattered on stone. A woman laughed—Lily's cadence, but warped, older.

"We should wake the others," Ethan said.

Deke spat. "And say what? That the spooks are feeling chatty?" He prodded Ethan's chest with the rifle barrel. "Get back by the fire 'fore you—"

Ethan.

Three voices now. Ma. Pa. And one that crooned in Blackfoot, vowels liquid as the creek under ice.

He walked.

Deke's curse followed him into the white. Frozen ferns crackled underboot. The compass burned hotter, its needle spinning wild. Shadows congealed ahead—a massive shape looming through the vapor.

"Easy pickings."

Ethan whirled. The mist parted to reveal a weathered trading post sign dangling from rusted chains. ***Crossroads. Dry Goods. Lead.*** Bloodred letters dripped down splintered wood.

A man leaned against the post. No—*through it*. Translucent fingers tamped tobacco into a pipe that shed no ash. "Your daddy begged prettier when the assayers came." The ghost's face rippled—stranger's features blurring into Pa's sun-ravaged smirk.

Ethan's hand closed on empty air where his revolver should've been. "You're not real."

"Real as the lead in your guts, boy." The specter's laugh became a death rattle. "That little valley you're chasing? Ain't sanctuary. It's a maw."

The compass sprang open, needle shearing off to impale the journal page in Ethan's mind—September's belladonna sketch. *Nightshade. Hallucinogen. Poison.*

"Bastard's bluffing." Ethan clenched the compass until brass edges drew blood. "Wind patterns. Temperature inversion creating auditory—"

Cold lips brushed his ear. "She screamed for you."

Ma's voice. Ma's grave-soil stench.

He ran.

Aspen trunks slapped his face. Mist coiled around his boots. Something howled—human? Wolf?—as he burst into camp.

Deke stood over the firepit, shoving a smoldering branch into the mist. "Took your damn time."

Clara rolled upright, Peacemaker sweeping the void. "Indians?"

"Worse." Lily knelt by the ashes, jade pendant spinning lazy circles above her cupped palm. "The land itself speaks here. Your mother knew." Her gaze hooked into Ethan. "Do you listen?"

The mist retreated as dawn's first blush scarred the east. Deke spat into the dying fire. "Next watch is yours, Blake. Try not to palaver with phantoms."

Ethan stared at the compass trembling in his hand. North quivered between two unfamiliar runes etched along the rim—symbols that hadn't been there yesterday.

Somewhere in the lightening woods, a twig snapped.

***

Ethan staggered back to the firepit, bootheels crunching pine needles louder than a drunk miner at confession. Dawn bled gray through the trees, but the mist clung like a jilted lover's perfume. His fingers found the compass again—cold brass biting into his palm, those fresh-carved runes throbbing against his skin like a second heartbeat.

"Christ's sake, Blake." Deke jabbed the smoldering branch toward the treeline. "You tryin' to get your fool scalp lifted?" The old tracker's shotgun lay broken over his arm, twin maws pointed at the retreating fog. "Next time them woods sing, you answer with lead, not questions."

Clara kicked dirt over the fire's last embers, her Peacemaker still out. "Mist don't stalk men. Not natural mist." She thumbed fresh rounds into the wheel. "You see eyes? Teeth?"

"Just voices." Ethan's knuckles whitened around the compass. "Ma's. Then... others."

Ligeia's jade pendant clinked against her belt flask as she crouched, pressing a palm to damp earth. "Land's restless. River stones upturned three days hence." Her nail traced a sigil in the mud that made Ethan's compass needle twitch. "Your mother's journals—they mention bloodroot blooming out of season?"

"Botanical notes, not ghost stories." Ethan flipped the journal open to September's pages. The belladonna sketch glared up, ink swirling like mist tendrils. "Temperature inversion. Hallucinogenic spores in fog. There's—"

A rifle shot cracked the morning.

All four ducked. Clara's pistol tracked westward where the report echoed. Deke spat black tobacco. "That was Sharps .50-110. Two miles off."

"Railroad guards," Clara muttered, holstering iron. "Or claim jumpers."

"Or worse." Lily stood, mud-smeared palm outstretched. A single ladybug crawled across her lifeline. "Men grow teeth when silver's involved."

The mist finally burned off, revealing aspens tattooed with old blaze marks. Ethan stared at the cryptic runes on his compass—same symbols now etched into nearby trunks. His gut churned. Every rational explanation crumbled like bad mortar.

Deke shouldered his shotgun. "Move out in five. Clara—scout that gunshot."

The Pinkerton nodded, melting into the pines without sound.

Lily pressed a canteen into Ethan's shaking hand. Her fingers brushed the fresh scar on his palm where the compass had bitten. "Spirits don't carve steel," she murmured. "But men do."

He drank. Bitter willowbark tea. "You believe it's real? This... Valley's Breath?"

Her laugh sounded like coins in a bone cup. "Believe the knife at your throat. The rest?" She tapped his journal. "Your mother believed enough for both of you."

Deke's boot connected with Ethan's saddlebags. "Quit jawin' and pack. Daylight's wasting."

As Ethan rolled his bedroll, his thumb found the journal's hidden compartment—the one with Ma's lock of hair and the bullet she'd died clutching. The copper casing felt warmer than it should. Somewhere north, thunder growled. Or maybe it was the mountain.

Didn't matter.

Truth waited in that valley whether it wanted company or not.

CHAPTER 6

Shadows of the Past

DEKE'S BOOT SANK INTO a mud pit that smelled like Satan's outhouse. He yanked it free with a *wet schlop*, spitting Copenhagen juice that stained the frost-bleached grass nicotine yellow. "Switchbacks," he growled, jerking chin toward the shale slope glittering with morning ice. "Half hour detour."

Clara's mare snorted as she pushed past, red bandana flapping like a battle standard. "Bullshit. Straight up's faster." Her gloved hand patted the revolver at her hip - new leather holster, same cocky gesture she'd used since stealing apples behind the livery at twelve.

Ethan watched the standoff through vaporized breath, fingers absently tracing his mother's compass tucked under three layers of wool. Deke's shoulders tensed beneath patched buckskin, that old Remington buffalo gun across his back catching first light. Clara was already knee-deep in frozen scrub, braid swinging like a pendulum counting down to disaster.

"Your funeral," Deke muttered when her mare's hooves sent a rockslide skittering downslope. A pine marten exploded from nearby brush, claws scrabbling on ice.

Clara wheeled her mount, cheeks apple-red under windburn. "Christ on a crutch, O'Sullivan! We ain't hauling grandmother's china. This ain't my first rodeo and sure as shit won't be my -"

Deke's arm shot out, callused palm smacking her mare's flank. The beast reared as six inches left of Clara's head erupted in splinters - the crack of a Sharps rifle echoing two heartbeats late.

"DOWN!" Ethan tackled Clara into a lichen-crusted depression as the second shot geysered mud where she'd stood. His elbow connected hard with her ribs. "Stay still, damn you!"

Deke's answering fire boomed like cathedral bells, peppering the ridge line with .45-70 fury. Powder smoke hung blue in the still air. Three more shots whined off granite - amateur hour from a nervous barrel. Ethan tasted blood where he'd bit his tongue.

"Posse?" Clara hissed, writhing like a landed trout beneath him.

"Worse." Deke spat, reloading with hands steady as anvils. "Townies."

The ambush ended as suddenly as it began, retreating hoofbeats drumming a staccato retreat. Clara shoved Ethan off with a grunt, thumbing fresh shells into her Colt. "Could've told me about the welcoming committee."

Deke's smile showed more gaps than teeth. "You were busy lecturing."

The mining camp found them three hours later when Deke's detour spit them into a bowl-shaped hollow. Ethan's boot sole flapped where shale had razor-bladed the leather. Clara's mare favored its left foreleg. Only Deke moved unchanged, eyes perpetually scanning the treeline.

"Hold." The tracker's arm barred their path like a railroad gate. His nostrils flared. "Iron rot. Quicklime."

The ruins emerged through skeletal birches - sagging cookshack devoured by wolf lichen, stamp mill gears frozen mid-scream. A ball-and-chain sat rusting beside what might've been a sluice ditch, now home to finger-length centipedes. Ethan crouched, brushing decades of pine duff from a brass plate still etched with LANGSTON HYDRAULIC CO.

Clara kicked a mummified rat skeleton. "Cheerful place."

Deke prowled the perimeter, sniffing like a coyote. "Three ways in. Four out. Ambushers circled back west." He paused at a collapsed adit, fingers tracing fresh scratches in the rotted timber. "Someone's been digging."

Ethan's compass needle twitched. Not north. He followed the pull past a dynamite shed missing its roof, past the arsenic-stained creekbed, to a cabin whose log walls listed like drunks. The door fell inward at his touch, releasing a century of trapped air that reeked of despair and spruce rot.

Inside, shadows clung thick as mourning crepe. Light spearing through bullet holes illuminated strange geometry - floorboards pried up and hastily replaced, a hearthstone sitting crooked. Ethan's bootheel caught the edge, revealing mouse-chewed papers beneath.

"Bingo." The brittle pages crackled like old skin. Faded script described timber yields, dynamite orders...and frantic margin notes about "the valley that drinks men." Ethan's pulse quickened. Mother's journals mentioned similar phrasing.

Outside, metal screeched. Clara's whoop split the silence. "Hey Professor! Check this motherlode!"

She straddled an overturned ore cart, grinning like she'd found El Dorado. At her feet lay a moss-caked skeleton still clutching a pickaxe. Gold fillings glinted in its jawbone smile.

Deke materialized from behind a boiler carcass, sleeve pressed over his nose. "Cyanide vats. Upwind."

Ethan barely heard. The journal entry in his hands spoke of Chinese workers disappearing into thin air, of "corpse lights" leading men off cliffs. Same stories Chief Looking Glass told around reservation campfires. Same madness that claimed his grandfather.

Wind moaned through the stamp mill's broken teeth. Somewhere east, a branch snapped. All three turned as one, weapons clearing leather in metallic chorus. The Ghost Walker's Dance swirled phantom fingers through the ruins, carrying the scent of snow and something older.

"Move out," Deke ordered. Not suggesting.

Clara opened her mouth. Closed it. For once.

***

The mining camp exhaled decay through collapsed ribs of timber. Lily crouched by a shattered assay office, gloved fingers sifting through rust-colored soil. Three feet away, Deke's bootprint sank deep where he'd kicked aside a rattlesnake. Her nostrils flared at the bitter almond stench wafting from the cyanide pits.

Something flickered in her peripheral vision—a cluster of bell-shaped flowers pushing through rotted floorboards. Her jade pendant warmed against her collarbone.

"Xīn yí..." She scrambled over splintered wood, medical satchel thumping against her hip. The plant's veined leaves pulsed faintly under her magnifying glass. Not just *Aconitum columbianum*, but something hybridized—petals shimmering with iridescent flecks like crushed beetles. Mother's journals mentioned this. *Valley's Breath mutation.*

Her scalpel flashed. Roots came up clinging to shards of blue glass— old poison bottles leaching into the soil. Perfect. Toxins forced adaptations. Back in San Francisco, the apothecary would pay six months' rent for three ounces of this. More importantly—she snapped off a leaf stem, watching milky sap bead—tetrodotoxin analogs could stabilize nervous tissue. Could let Kai walk again without seizures.

Across the clearing, Ethan wiped soot from a ledger page. The cabin's remaining wall groaned as wind punched through bullet holes.

March 12th, 1872. Crew refuses to dig west slope. Claims "shadow people" guard the lode. Hired replacement workers from Canton—no such superstitions.

His thumb smeared the next entry.

April 3rd. Forty men vanished overnight. Tools left standing as if dropped mid-swing. Found O'Reilly's coat...empty. Like snake shedding skin. Board votes to abandon claim.

The spine crackled when he flipped it. A folded map fluttered out—terrain markings matching his mother's sketches. Red Xs marked cave mouths along Ghostwalker Ridge. One labeled in shaky script: WHERE THEY TOOK THE BOY.

Metal screeched outside. Ethan's Spencer carbine came up as Clara ducked through the doorway. "Christ, Professor. You planning to read us bedtime stories?" She kicked a mummified rat across the room. "Camp's crawling with enough arsenic to drop a buffalo. Deke says move."

He pocketed the journal. "Your opinion?"

"That skeleton by the sluice gate? Gold caps still on his teeth." She spun her Colt onto one finger. "Man died rich and stupid. My kinda epitaph."

***

Deke built the fire like he did everything—methodical, no wasted motion. Frost crept down from the peaks, biting through wool coats. Lily ground her new specimen with a mortar, the rhythmic crunch syncopating with Clara whittling stakes from lodgepole pine.

Ethan tossed another log on the flames. "Cold enough to freeze the balls off a brass monkey."

"Forty below last winter." Deke's knife scraped black gunk from a jackrabbit haunch. "Old Man Clancy bet his nephew five dollars to lick a shovel. Took the kid's tongue clean off."

Clara snorted. "Bullshit."

"Found the shovel come spring. Still had skin stuck to it."

"Jesus, Deke." Lily didn't look up from her pestle. "Some of us are eating."

The fire popped. Sparks swirled up to die in the dark. Deke stared into the coals. "Was sixteen when I killed my first man."

Clara froze mid-whittle. Ethan kept stirring the coffee tin like they were discussing crop rotations.

"County sheriff caught me boosting chickens." Deke's blade sawed through gristle. "Said he'd hang Pa instead if I didn't sign confession. Handed me the pen..." He flung the gutted rabbit on a flat rock. "Bastard's head made this wet thump hitting the cell bars. Like melon dropped from hayloft."

Lily's grinding stopped. Pine sap hissed in the flames.

"Rode with Quantrill's boys after that." He spat into the fire. "You wanted to know why I quit? Kansas farmhouse. Girl hiding under porch stairs. Had this doll..." His calloused thumb rubbed the rifle stock. "Made from corn husks. Eyes were buttons off some banker's waistcoat."

Ethan poured coffee into a dented tin cup. Passed it over. "How old?"

"Eight. Maybe nine." Deke drank deep, not flinching at the boil. "That's when you see it clear—outlaw's just a wolf other wolves hate. Time to find new woods."

The wind shifted. Somewhere in the pines, branches clattered like dice. Clara stood abruptly. "First watch." Her boots crunched toward the tree line, revolver already drawn.

Lily stood, brushing powdered aconite from her skirt. "I'll...check the perimeter specimens." Her lamp vanished into the aspens, leaving trembling shadows.

Ethan waited seven full breaths. "Quantrill's dead. That girl's probably got grandkids now." He poked the fire. Embers swarmed upward. "You ever think about writing them?"

Deke's shoulders stiffened. "What's there to say?"

"Start with 'I'm sorry.' End with 'Name your price.'" Ethan threw the last biscuit into the flames. "Or keep riding circles. Your choice."

A long silence. Then Deke's rasping chuckle. "You're a shit preacher, Blake."

"Yeah." Ethan stretched out his bedroll. "But I'm warm company."

Overhead, the aurora borealis writhed green. Somewhere beyond the ridge, a wolf howled. Deke sat staring at the dying fire until the stars burned cold.

Aiyana Whitefeather counted seven distinct lies in the smoke.

Her fingers brushed the red bead woven into her braid—one for each season she'd kept this valley's secrets. Below the ridge, the white men's fire spat gray splinters skyward. False prayers. The wind brought her whispers of aconite and gun oil, desperation masquerading as purpose.

"Three warriors, one healer," she murmured to the spruce waxwing perched on her knee. The bird cocked head, black eyes reflecting campfire glints. "And the leader...broken but mending." Her thumb traced the bear claw necklace beneath her buckskin tunic. Foreigners never understood how flames confessed truths—the nervous flicker when Clara checked her revolvers, the sullen smolder mirroring Deke's hunched shoulders.

The waxwing took flight as metal clanked below. Aiyana stilled. The big one—Ethan—stood staring directly at her hiding place. She didn't breathe until he turned back to poking the fire. Good eyes. Dangerous.

She left three strands of sweetgrass tied with wolf fur where she'd been crouching. Let them find that tomorrow. If they were worthy.

***

Victor Langston's pocket watch clicked open. Three minutes late. The train whistle screamed its cheap apology as he stepped onto Whiterock's splintered platform. His crocodile boots sank into fresh manure.

"Charming."

He scraped shit off sole against a hitching post, eyeing the sheriff's office across the street. Two drunks slumped outside Hartley's General Store tracked his movements like rheumy-eyed bloodhounds. Victor smiled. Their heads snapped forward.

The stationmaster scurried over, cap twisting in grease-stained hands. "Mr. Langston! Your trunks—"

"Burn them." Victor tossed his rail ticket into the dirt. "The dust alone warrants arson."

He crossed Main Street at funeral pace, silver-topped cane tapping irregular rhythm. Let them stare. Let them whisper. The bank's new vault door gleamed through dusty windows—his first stop tomorrow. But today...

Sheriff Sam Hart leaned against his office doorway, coffee steaming in chipped enamel mug. "Heard you bought up half the county's timber rights."

"My accountant handles small change." Victor's cane tip pressed into bootheel grooves worn into the boardwalk. "I prefer investing in men."

"Careful investment?"

"Liquid assets." Victor's smile showed teeth. "Men who understand civilization flows westward on twin rivers—capital and lead."

The sheriff's gaze dropped to Victor's Colt Peacemaker. Ivory grip. Nickel-plated. Obscenely out of place. "Heard that same speech before Quantrill burned Lawrence."

"History's written by account holders, Sheriff." Victor removed his gloves one finger at a time. "Shall we review your ledger?"

***

Inside, flyspecked wanted posters fluttered as Victor shut the door. He claimed the single visitor's chair without invitation. Sam remained standing behind his desk—strategic elevation.

"Blake's party left eight days ago." Victor sniffed. The room stank of sweat and blackpowder. "Hired a known outlaw as guide. You've filed no charges."

"Montana's not a state yet." Sam thumbed open a warrant book. "Federal marshals handle—"

"Irrelevant." Victor placed a gold double eagle on the desk. The coin spun, catching thin light. "What did Blake take?"

Sam's boot heel ground tobacco shreds into floorboards. "Prospecting gear. Standard—"

"Standard?" Victor added second coin. Their chime sang counterpoint to the sheriff's swallowed curse. "No one risks Blackfoot territory for 'standard.'"

The third eagle gleamed between them. Sam's jaw worked. "Freight manifest showed...surveyor's chains. Sextant. Preserved specimens jars."

Victor's smile tasted like arsenic. "Mining claims require neither astronomy nor biology." He stood abruptly. Chair legs shrieked. "Keep the coins. Buy yourself civilization."

At the door, he paused. "Oh—send Deputy Wilkins to the hotel later. I've questions about his sister's...medical debts."

Sam's coffee mug cracked against the wall as Victor stepped into afternoon glare. Behind him, muffled through clapboard walls: "Goddamn carrion crow!"

Victor adjusted his cuffs. Carrion fed empires.

***

Aiyana watched the stars bleed together—white scratches on obsidian. The white men's camp lay silent now except for the healer's mutters. She chewed bitterroot, spitting pulp into palm.

Four possible paths tomorrow. Northwest led to false springs. East, the cliff bears' nesting grounds. Southwest...

Her fingers found the new scar on her forearm—pale flesh raised during last moon's vision quest. The elder's warning rasped in memory: *Fire eyes coming. Steel wings.*

Dawn wind stirred the sweetgrass offering she'd left. None had touched it. Not yet blind.

She melted into tree shadows as the first wolf howled. Let them face a few tests before the real trials began.

Chapter 7

Nature's Fury

T HE SKY PRESSED DOWN like a bruised fist as Deke led the party through a maze of lodgepole pines. Needles crunched underfoot, releasing sharp medicinal scents that did fuck-all to cut the metallic tang gathering in the air. He clocked the shift before the others—the way the aspen leaves flipped their silver undersides upward in silent supplication. A guttural roll of thunder echoed off the Sawtooth Peaks to the west.

"Step lively," Deke growled, adjusting the pack digging into his shoulders. "Storm's coming in hungry."

Ethan wiped sweat from his brow, the Blake family compass thumping against his chest with each step. "Thought you said we'd beat the weather."

"Thought wrong." Deke scanned the ridgeline where raven flocks abandoned their perches in sudden unison. His right hand drifted to the old knife scar beneath his shirt—a phantom ache from a Cheyenne arrowhead that always flared when trouble brewed. The wind shifted, carrying the unmistakable musk of charged silt. First rule of mountain storms: never argue with their timing.

Lily Chen paused to secure her specimen case, rain droplets jeweled in her black braids. "Barometric pressure's dropping faster than a whore's —"

"Save the poetry," Deke snapped. "That shelf cloud's gonna unzip any minute. Move or get flash-flooded."

The party lurched into a ragged jog just as the sky ripped open. Quarter-sized raindrops exploded against granite slabs, turning game trails into caramel-colored slurries. Deke's boots skidded across lichen-slick boulders, his mind mapping the terrain through decades of muscle memory—jagged outcrops here, unstable scree slopes there. No caves. No overhangs. Fuck-all for shelter except...

There. Between two finger-like spires of sandstone. A slit in the earth barely wider than a coffin.

"Gully!" Deke barked, jabbing a calloused finger toward the crevice. "Tight squeeze but it's stone-dry above the wash line. Mostly."

Mostly had to fucking suffice.

The deluge became biblical as they scrambled downward. Hailstones ricocheted off Ethan's leather satchel, denting the brass buckles. Lily's rolled maps bled indigo ink across her fingers. Every slip in the mud drew curses swallowed by thunderclaps that shook marrow. Deke moved like a man possessed—planting boots sideways for traction, hauling stragglers by their collar straps when needed. His green eyes catalogued dangers in flickering lightning strobes: unstable boulders trembling in their mud nests, chokeberry bushes disguising drop-offs, the telltale gurgle of runoff gaining power.

"Christ alive, it's a goddamn waterslide!" Tommy Reynolds yelped as his boot soles hydroplaned across clay.

Deke caught the kid's arm before he face-planted into a prickly pear cluster. "Waterslide don't try to kill you. This does."

The canyon mouth welcomed them with a spit of gravel. Deke shoved bodies inward like counting sheep—eight, nine, ten—before the arroyo behind them roared to life. A chocolate-brown torrent exploded down the gulch, chewing through fifty years' worth of sediment in seconds.

"Higher!" Deke bellowed over the cacophony. The narrow defile became a kaleidoscope of chaos—backpacks bouncing off walls, elbows knocking rock, everyone scrambling over the geological equivalent of a giant's jawbone. He spotted the shelf first: a weathered limestone lip six feet up the east wall. Dry. For now.

"Boost 'em up," Deke ordered, interlacing his fingers into a stirrup. Mud-streaked faces blurred past as he hoisted each explorer to relative safety. Lily went first without protest, her practical boots finding purchase in the limestone's pockmarks. Ethan hesitated—pride or stupidity, hard to tell—until Deke nearly dislocated the bastard's shoulder shoving him upward.

The shelf proved tighter than a preacher's asshole. Shoulders pressed together like tobacco plugs in a tin. Below, the flood churned with tree carcasses and the bloated corpse of a mule deer. Deke wedged himself between a shale column and the group, feeling the rock vibrate with the current's fury.

"Cozy," Lily deadlocked, peeling a banana slug from her sleeve.

Ethan stared at the tomb-like walls. "How long?"

"Till the creek forgets its anger." Deke pulled a skinning knife to clean mud from his boot treads. "Hour. Three. Depends how much piss the clouds still got."

A particularly vicious current slammed a pine trunk into their perch. The impact sent shale shrapnel flying.

"Christ!" Tommy shielded his face. "We're sitting ducks here!"

Deke spat a stream of tobacco juice into the maelstrom. "Ducks float. You'd sink." He nodded toward Ethan's clenched fist. "Quit strangling that compass unless you want its needle busted."

Silence settled like gunpowder residue. Rain sheeted across the canyon's open roof, creating a spectral curtain that blurred the outside world. Deke watched the waterline inch upward—an inch every seven minutes by his count. Not great. Not terminal. Yet.

Lily extracted a brass pocket gauge from her kit. "Current velocity's increased twelve percent since we climbed up."

"Noticed." Deke repositioned to block a spray of debris. His lower back screamed from the awkward angle. Didn't matter. Men had died comfortable—he'd take aching muscles over a watery grave any day.

The compass around Ethan's neck caught a lightning burst. "You've seen worse."

"Once." Deke's jaw tightened. "Buried three men after."

Another log cannonballed past. The shelf trembled.

"Cheerful bastard," Tommy muttered.

Deke let the insult hang. Let them think him cruel. Fear kept idiots alive.

By the time the water crested—two fingers below the limestone lip— the storm had stolen all sense of day from night. Deke kept watch through the deluge's remaining dregs, tracking debris patterns like tea leaves in a cup. When the first cricket dared chirp, he finally unstiffened his legs.

"Move out slow," he ordered, lowering himself into knee-deep muck. "Current's sleeping but the bottom's still mean."

The canyon spat them back into a world scrubbed raw—trees gleaming like exposed bones, every raindrop glittering in post-storm light. Deke didn't relax until he'd scouted fifty yards upstream. Found what he expected: fresh landslide scars, relocated boulders, nature's furniture rearranged.

He turned to the bedraggled party. "Rest here. Next push's harder."

As the others collapsed onto relatively dry stones, Deke scaled a nearby promontory. Let them think he was scouting trails. Truth was, he needed distance from their grateful stares. Redemption didn't come from playing hero—came from surviving another day with fewer ghosts.

The compass in his pocket felt heavier than usual. Deke fished it out, watching the needle quiver. North had shifted three degrees since morning. Storms changed more than landscapes.

He pocketed the tool. Let tomorrow worry about new directions. Today had demanded enough.

***

The canyon walls pressed close, rainwater still cascading down striated rock like liquid guilt. Tommy Reynolds' thumb kept worrying the Colt's hammer spur, the nickel plating catching what little light squeezed through slate-colored clouds overhead.

"Quit fingering that iron," Deke growled without turning around. "Unless you aim to polish it into a nub."

Tommy's laugh came out shriller than he intended. "Just keeping her dry's all." The lie curdled in his mouth. Every shadow between the boulders seemed to twitch—phantom shapes that might be crouching men or just storm-shook scrub oak. His boot slipped on algae-slick stone, and the gun barked before he knew he'd drawn, the report echoing like cannon fire between narrowing walls.

Lily Chen didn't flinch. She was elbow-deep in a crevice, retrieving sodden supply sacks with the clinical focus of a surgeon. "Lead composition?" she asked, shaking water from a canvas bundle.

Ethan blinked rain from his lashes. "Pardon?"

"The bullet that nearly parted my hair. Seventy-eight percent lead? Sixty?" Her fingers kept working knots loose. "Asking for my incident report."

Tommy's throat worked. "Wasn't aiming at—"

"Ninety-two percent." Lily produced a damp notebook, its pages swollen with moisture. "Commercial cartridges favor softer alloys. Helps prevent barrel fouling." She finally looked up, dark eyes sharp as obsidian flakes. "Also makes them useless against granite, in case you were curious."

Ethan found himself biting back a grin. The botanist's collar hung open where a button had torn free, jade pendant gleaming against rain-sheened skin. He tossed her a length of braided cord from his pack. "Try this with the ration crate."

59

Their fingers brushed during the exchange—brief as a hummingbird's wingbeat—and something passed between them more tangible than hemp fibers. Not attraction, precisely. Recognition. Two minds clicking through a shared problem like gears in his mother's old chronometer.

Tommy wasn't having it. "Y'all acting mighty cozy considering we're one lightning strike from becoming charcoal briquettes!" His voice skated up an octave. "That symbol carved in the—"

Deke materialized behind him, a dripping specter. "Ain't no symbols. Ain't no phantom trackers. Just your lizard brain pissing itself." He flicked the Colt's barrel downward. "Holster that before you ventilate someone worth mourning."

The storm redoubled its fury as night fell, transforming their meager overhang into a thunderous drum. Ethan took first watch, back against cold stone as others bedded down on shale fragments that grudgingly passed for bedding. Lily's breathing steadied first—measured inhalations that synced with the rasp of her whetstone across a harvesting knife. Tommy's came in staccato bursts between whispered prayers to saints and saloon girls.

Sleep took Ethan like a garrote.

***

He stood atop a basalt column beneath alien stars. The air tasted of copper and burnt honey. Below stretched a valley choked with mist that moved against the wind—swirling patterns suggesting colossal figures striding through fog. On the farthest peak, backlit by a greenish aurora, stood a man with Ethan's jawline and a cavalry coat bleached bone-white by decades.

"Look down," his father's voice boomed without moving lips.

The mist parted. A thousand feet below, spectral miners swung picks at a mountainside that wept black blood. Each strike echoed like a funeral bell. Among them, tiny as ants, walked a woman cradling journals against her chest. Ethan's throat closed. He knew that determined stride anywhere.

"Mama?"

The vision dissolved into suffocating dark filled with the scent of turned earth and lily roots. Something cold pressed against his palm—a stone tablet etched with symbols that squirmed under his touch. A voice that wasn't a voice thrummed in his marrow: *Find the leylines before they bleed dry.*

***

Ethan woke choking on daylight. The storm had scoured the sky into a hard cerulean bowl, leaving the world smelling of wet pine and pending trouble. Lily's bootprints circled their camp in overlapping spirals—mapping safe paths through the debris-choked wash. She paused now, head cocked toward distant scree slopes where fresh landslides glistened like unhealed wounds.

"Dreams or premonitions?" She didn't look over as Ethan approached, but her hand drifted to the jade pendant.

He scooped a shard of quartz from the mud. "My mother used to say there's no difference west of the Missouri." The stone felt alive in his palm—vibrations humming up his arm bones. "You believe in spiritual magnetism?"

"Believe in patterns." Her finger traced an aerial root dangling from a battered box elder. "This survived winds that stripped century oaks bare. Because it bent instead of fought." She finally met his gaze. "Your father's up there?"

The question landed between them like a lit fuse. Somewhere downstream, Deke was cursing at a mule refusing to cross the newly altered creekbed. Tommy's voice rose in nervous laughter that set Ethan's teeth on edge.

"Up there." Ethan nodded toward peaks crowned with lingering stormclouds. "Down here. Everywhere except where he damn well ought to be." The quartz bit his palm. "You think that's crazy."

Lily unsheathed her knife, tested the edge against a strand of hair that divided itself silently. "My great-grandfather walked from Guangzhou to Beijing with nothing but silk maps and poetry carved into his walking staff." She nodded at the pendant. "Family tradition says he followed the jade's heartbeat." A rare smile flickered. "Got arrested six times for trespassing imperial reserves. Your kind of crazy runs in better circles."

They broke camp wordlessly after that, but Ethan caught her studying him when she thought he wasn't looking—the way she might examine some rare hybrid sprouting between expected lineages. Tommy's hands still shook, but now they did it quietly, fingers compulsively checking each cartridge before reloading. Deke watched everything and said nothing, which somehow cut deeper than any accusation.

The trail ahead switchbacked violently, exposing raw earth where the storm had ripped away vegetation. As they climbed, Ethan kept glancing back at the canyon shrinking below—its once-imposing walls reduced to a scar in the landscape. Lily's words looped in his skull, finding purchase in cracks he'd thought long sealed.

Patterns, not ghosts. Leylines instead of absolution. Maybe redemption wasn't a destination, but a path laid stone by stolen stone. The quartz fragment burned in his pocket, or maybe that was just sunlight finally breaking through.

***

The mud smelled like old coins and burnt gunpowder. Ethan came awake with a jolt, fingers already clawing at the cold sludge caking his left cheek. Dawn light bled through the canyon's eastern notch, revealing the symbol pressed into the earth beside his bedroll—three concentric circles bisected by a jagged line. Exactly like the sketch on page 137 of his mother's journals. *The valley marks its own.*

"Christ alive," he muttered, scrambling for his pack. Gravel bit through his damp shirt as he dragged out Sarah Blake's weathered notebook. The pages stuck together until he wiped his hand clean on trouser wool. There —smudged charcoal rendering from 1862, same configuration beneath her notation: *Sighted near Black Coulee spring. J.B. insists compass true north deviates here. Possible mineral interference?*

Lily's shadow fell across the mud glyph before her boots did. "Your ghost left a love note?" She crouched, jade pendant swinging free of her collar. Her index finger hovered above the symbol without touching it. "That's no erosion pattern."

"Not unless erosion reads mother's field notes." Ethan thrust the journal at her. "She documented this exact mark thirty years back. Same formation, same..."

The words died as Lily's nail traced air above the central bisecting line. "This fracture here—see how it aligns with the canyon wall striations? Your mother was mapping geological faults."

A rifle bolt snapped behind them. Tommy stood ten paces off, breath fogging the morning chill as he stared down his Winchester's barrel at nothing. "Movement," he rasped. "North ridge."

Deke materialized from the rocks above, scattering pebbles. "Mule deer. Three point buck." He spat tobacco juice that stained the mud black. "Quickshot here's fixing to ruin breakfast."

Ethan snapped the journal shut. "We need to—"

"Move," Deke finished. He jerked his chin westward where the canyon narrowed. "Storm's reshaped the throat. Got maybe two hours before runoff turns that gulch to quicksand."

They climbed over carcasses of lightning-split pines. The canyon's upper reaches bore fresh scars—boulders perched like broken teeth in raw earth, stream beds rerouted through shattered stone. Lily paused where the path bifurcated, squinting at lichen patterns on adjacent cliffs.

"West fork," Deke called without turning. "East slope's rotten with widowmakers."

Tommy's laugh came out shrill. "Sure. Because west looks so goddamn hospitable." He kicked a mangled tin cup wedged between roots—some forty-niner's lost supper. The clatter sent rock doves bursting from a crevice.

Ethan caught Lily's arm as she bent to examine a peculiar moss growth. "You feel that?"

Her pulse jumped under his grip. "The tremor? Started twenty minutes back. Harmonic resonance from underground water flows."

"If you two want to hold hands, do it walking." Deke didn't break stride. "Ground's unstable past the choke point."

The canyon spat them out onto a slope of scree that hadn't existed yesterday. Below sprawled a nightmare diorama of the valley they'd traversed three days prior—cottonwoods uprooted like matchsticks, river channels boiled dry, and where the main trail had switchbacked up Sentinel Ridge now yawned a granite gash oozing ochre sludge.

Tommy sat down hard. "Well... fuck."

Deke unsheathed his bowie knife and began scratching lines in a flat stone. "Langston's Folly mine's still northwest. Two options—hug the new fissure's east rim or backtrack through the avalanche zone."

Lily produced a brass clinometer from her pack. "East rim's shale composition. We'd need pitons and—"

"We don't have pitons," Deke said.

"—or," she continued, shooting him a look colder than the spring-fed pools dotting the slope, "we follow the mineral deposits." She pointed to rust-colored streaks veining the fissure walls. "Iron oxide trails. Leads straight to Langston's silver veins."

Ethan studied Deke's stone map—crude but accurate. "Backtracking adds half a day. My father's last camp was..."

"Three miles past Langston's." Deke sheathed his knife. "Choice is yours, Blake."

The wind shifted, carrying the metallic tang of distant rain. Somewhere below, boulders groaned against their new arrangements. Tommy picked at his trigger guard, muttering about Comancheros and Spanish gold curses.

Lily stepped to the fissure edge, pendant cupped in her palm. "Chen family rule number seven—when the mountain breaks your path, walk its bones." She began uncoiling rope from her pack.

Ethan met Deke's stare. "East rim."

The tracker's beard twitched. "Best check your bootlaces."

They moved single-file along the precipice. Halfway across, the shale began singing—a low hum that vibrated through boot soles. Lily paused, pressing her ear to a rust-stained boulder.

"Sandstone layers grinding," she announced. "Harmless."

Tommy wasn't convinced. "Tell that to my—"

The ledge collapsed under his left foot.

Ethan lunged, catching Tommy's pack strap as the younger man scrabbled for purchase. For three heartbeats they hung suspended over air that reeked of crushed pyrite—Tommy's wild eyes reflecting the abyss below, Ethan's shoulder screaming as it took the full weight. Then Deke's rawhide whip snaked out, wrapping Tommy's wrist in a brutal embrace.

Between curses and leverage, they hauled him back. Tommy lay gasping on solid ground, fingers clawing dirt like a man resurrected. Lily already had her kit open, mixing something that smelled of pine tar and regret.

"Drink." She shoved a tin cup at him. "It'll steady the hands."

Deke examined his whip for damage. "Next slip costs you a finger."

Ethan flexed his aching shoulder, staring northwest where Langston's ruined smokestacks jutted from the raped hillside. The symbol from dawn haunted him—three circles, one truth. Somewhere beyond that broken horizon, James Blake's bones waited with answers. And whatever else the valley had buried, it was stirring.

The canyon spat them out onto a slope of mud-glazed shale that glittered like broken liquor bottles. Ethan's boots sank knuckle-deep with every step, the earth still weeping stormwater. He adjusted the leather strap of his mother's satchel—the one holding her journals and the Blake Wayfinder Set—feeling the brass compass dig into his ribcage through the damp wool shirt.

"Hold." Deke's whip cracked air two inches from Tommy's ear. "Step where I step, pup. This ain't a church social."

Tommy glared but matched the older man's bootprints exactly. Lily crouched upstream, fingers splayed against a vein of quartz running through the mud. "Iron deposits here," she called. "Compasses'll lie like cheating husbands."

Ethan nodded, unbuttoning his shirt to retrieve the jade pendant warm against his chest. "Chen family trick?"

"Grandmother's parlor game." She flicked pine resin from her nails. "Find true north using lichen patterns when the miners got themselves lost in—"

"—In the whiskey fog of '78," Deke finished, spitting tobacco. "Heard the tale. You gonna mystic us a path or what?"

Lily's smile carried knives. She pressed three foxglove leaves into Ethan's palm—purple edges curling like dead men's fingers. "Chew these when the vertigo hits. Slope's unstable as Tommy's trigger discipline."

The sharpshooter flushed, hand drifting to his holstered Remington. "I didn't—"

"You did." Deke scuffed a boot along a scree-filled crevice. "Blake! How's that book learnin' match up?"

Ethan spread his mother's map across a flat rock, weighting corners with river stones. The ink had bled during the storm, transforming mountain peaks into Rorschach smears. But the symbol he'd found at dawn—three concentric circles etched in mud—glowed fresh behind his eyelids. Same as the margin sketch on page 117 of her journals. Same as his father's belt buckle in the single surviving daguerreotype.

"Langston's old rail spur." Ethan traced a vanished line on the map. "If we cut across the Slide Iron Gorge..."

Deke snorted. "Gorge is soup. Storm carved a new river through it." He tapped the jade pendant with his whip handle. "Your magic rock say anything useful?"

The pendant's warmth pulsed once—a heartbeat Ethan felt in his molars. He turned slowly, boots squelching, until the carved surface chilled against his skin. "Northwest. Through the widowmakers."

Ponderosa skeletons loomed ahead, root systems clawing at air where the landslide had undercut the ridge. Tommy paled. "Those pines're hanging by spit and spite."

"Spit, spite, and three dollars' worth of Chinese explosives." Lily hoisted her pack, revealing six red paper tubes tucked in the straps. "Courtesy of Uncle Bao's fireworks stall."

Deke grinned for the first time in three days.

They moved like a single organism—Ethan navigating via pendulum swings of the cooling jade, Deke scouting footholds in the rotten shale, Lily rigging charges with surgeon's precision. Even Tommy proved useful, scaling a precariously leaning pine to secure climbing ropes.

"Fire in the hole!" Lily yanked the fuse cord.

The blast cracked the mountainside's voicebox. Ethan tasted saltpetre and ancestral ghosts as the widowmakers collapsed into a splintered bridge across the gorge. He shoved foxglove between cheek and gum, the bitter sap neutralizing the sway in his knees.

Deke tested the log jam with his weight. "Cross quick before the spirits get pissy."

Halfway over, Tommy froze. The splinters beneath his boots groaned like a tortured fiddle. Below, the makeshift river belched up the stench of exposed coal seams.

"Don't look down," Ethan ordered.

"Kinda have to," Tommy whispered, right boot sliding. "There's... Jesus, there's bones in the water."

Lily crouched, skirts be damned. "Oxen carcasses from the '65 freight disaster. Perfectly normal."

"Normal?" Tommy's laugh bordered on hysterical. "That skull just winked at me!"

Deke's whip snapped past Tommy's ear, severing a spiderweb. "Move or make room for someone who will."

They reached solid ground as the log bridge dissolved into the rapids. Ethan spat out mangled foxglove, the lingering numbness making his tongue feel borrowed. Lily uncorked her canteen.

"Drink. The water's steeped with—"

"—Let me guess." Deke swiped it. "Mystic valley mojo?"

"Peppermint and willow bark. For the clenching." She nodded at Ethan's white-knuckled grip on the jade pendant.

Night fell hard as a gambler's debt. They camped in the lee of boulders striated like prison bars. Ethan volunteered for first watch, claiming he needed to chart their course. Truth was, the three circles burned behind his eyes whenever he blinked—the mud symbol, the journal sketch, his father's ghost in that damn dream pointing toward mountains that bled silver.

He opened the oldest journal, its pages crackling with dried riverweed. Moonlight caught his mother's marginalia: *J.B. believed the Legion's secret lay where three rivers marry. But rivers lie. Follow the breath.*

The pendant throbbed once against his chest. Below camp, the newly born river muttered over bones and rocks. Somewhere beyond the next ridge, the Valley's Breath stirred the pines into whispering conspiracies.

Tommy's snore hitched mid-rumble. Deke stood silhouetted against the moonlit gorge, coiled whip catching starlight. Lily slept sitting upright, her diagnostic kit open like a hymnal.

Ethan folded the journal shut. Dawn would find them in the shadow of the Sentinel Range, where storms bred faster than sin and the Ghost Walker's Dance twisted through ravines. His father's bones waited in that unmapped cathedral of stone.

So did answers that might turn a son's hunger into grief.

He took first watch anyway.

CHAPTER 8

Crossroads

THE MAP CRACKLED UNDER Ethan's calloused fingers like dried snake skin. He anchored its corners with three river stones worn smooth by generations of runoff, the Blake family compass gleaming dully beside a sketched-in canyon. "Northwest trail follows the old Blackfoot hunting paths," he said, tracing a frayed ink line with his bowie knife. "But Langston's crew reported three cave-ins along that stretch last monsoon."

Deke spat a stream of tobacco juice that hit a thistle growing between the wagon ruts. "Safer than playing hopscotch across crumbling mesas." His eyes never stopped moving - tracking a red-tailed hawk's spirals, measuring the angle of afternoon light through lodgepole pines. The Sharps rifle slung across his back shifted as he turned toward Clara. "You ain't the one digging lead out of people when shit goes sideways."

Clara kicked a pinecone into the dust, her Remington derringer catching sunlight as she gestured. "Thompson's Gulch route puts us two days ahead of schedule. Unless you're getting soft, old man." She thumbed the hammer back on pure reflex, cylinder rotating with a lethal clockwork click. At twenty-three, she carried herself like a cocked pistol - all compressed energy and hair-trigger impatience.

Lily's fingernails dug crescent moons into her palms. The jade pendant between her collarbones pulsed warm as forge coals, though no sunlight touched it. Her gaze fixed on the distant ridgline where the Ghost Walker's Dance swirled in defiance of prevailing winds. "The land's speaking," she murmured, more to the bristlecone pine sapling at her feet than to the others. "Can't you—"

Hoofbeats cut her off. Twelve riders materialized from the quaking aspens, Henry Thompson leading with the careless arrogance of a man who owned dynamite shares in hell. His sorrel mare sidestepped a gopher hole, tack jingling like a saloon girl's bracelet. "Blake! Heard you were sniffing around the Sentinel passes." Thompson's grin showed too many teeth, the scar through his left eyebrow twisting like a barbed wire tattoo. "My boys could use a cartographer who doesn't piss himself at the first wolf howl."

Ethan's knuckles went white around his knife hilt. He counted six Springfield rifles glinting among Thompson's crew, two pack mules laden with blasting gel cases. The Blake Wayfinder Set's brass levels trembled on the map stone, detecting vibrations no human ear could catch.

Deke shifted position, boots scuffing dirt in deliberate arcs that cleared his firing lanes. His green eyes locked onto a broad-shouldered rider chewing sassafras root - the man's holster tied low and smooth as a Mississippi cardsharp's. Lily edged closer to Deke's blind side, her hand brushing the bone handle of her herb knife. The pendant's heat spiked when Thompson's gaze lingered on Clara's ammunition belt.

"Your timber crews still using Chinese powder monkeys on the Bitterroot line?" Ethan's voice carried the deceptive calm of ice over rapids. He palmed the compass, its needle swinging wildly before stabilizing on true north. "Heard the Last Chance Mine's breathing fumes that'd choke a sulfur geyser."

Thompson's laugh barked across the clearing. "Progress ain't a Sunday picnic. But combine your maps with my..." He patted a cylindrical survey case slung behind his saddle. "...modern methods, we'll carve through those mesa walls like Christmas cake."

A whiskey jack's shrill cry split the air. Lily's head snapped toward the swirling ground fog now creeping across the crossroads. It flowed against the wind, tendrils curling like question marks around the horses' fetlocks. Her lips formed silent words in Mandarin - a childhood rhyme about foxes that steal greedy men's shadows.

Deke's bootheel ground a pebble to powder. "Funny." He spit again, closer to Thompson's mare this time. "Last fellas I saw carrying Breckenridge gelignite ended up decorating a Paiute burial tree." His thumb hovered near the Sharps' hammer, calculating drop rates and powder burns across twenty yards of open ground.

***

The whiskey jack's cry still hung in the air when Clara's boot caught on a root. She stumbled sideways into Lily, fingers digging into the other woman's sleeve. "Christ on a cracker," she hissed, voice cracking like thin ice. "That's *Jasper Bloody O'Sullivan* leaning on Thompson's pack mule."

Every head snapped toward the man adjusting a survey tripod. Silver-capped teeth flashed beneath a waxed mustache as he tipped his hat. "Little Clara Benson?" Jasper drawled. "Last I saw you, you were knee-deep in stable muck trying to -"

Deke's Sharps hit the dirt before the click of his hammer registered. He took three strides forward, spurs singing death metal. The scar along his jaw pulsed crimson. "You rotting son of a -"

Memories ambushed him. Jasper's laugh echoing through burning timber. The way their father's Remington had felt warm in his palm that last morning. Copper-tang blood mixing with spring runoff.

Ethan's hand clamped Deke's shoulder. "Stand down." The order carried the weight of river ice creaking underfoot. His other hand tightened around the Blake compass, its brass edges biting flesh.

Thompson's men outnumbered them two-to-one, and that Breckenridge gelignite could level the pass.

Clara's knuckles whitened around her Winchester. "He stole my best mare! Swore it was a stud fee then sold her to Fort Peck slaughterhouse!"

Lily's herbs rustled in the sudden silence. The ground fog thickened around Jasper's polished boots as he smirked. "Technically, darlin', that was your daddy's -"

A pebble pinged off Jasper's temple. Deke flexed his throwing hand, voice gravel dragged through broken glass. "Next one goes down your throat."

Thompson stepped between the brothers, leather gloves creaking as he spread his hands. "Now gentlemen, surely -"

Ethan's compass needle spun wildly before locking northeast. The map against his thigh showed the safer route looping past Blackfoot burial grounds. But the direct path... His mother's journal entries swam behind his eyes - *Three Sisters Terraces visible only when the Breath dances.*

Above them, ponderosa needles began to shiver. Not from wind.

Lily tilted her face upward first. "Qi guai..."

The Valley's Breath unfurled across the twilight like God's own barbed wire. Ribbons of jade and mercury twisted through the pines, painting everyone's skin corpse-pale. Deke's scar turned phosphorescent. Somewhere down the ridge, a wolf howled in discordant harmony with the shimmering air.

Jasper crossed himself. Thompson's men stumbled back, one dropping his canteen to clutch a turquoise amulet. Even the horses stilled, ears flat as the lights reflected in their wide, dark eyes.

Clara exhaled a half-laugh. "Well shit. Ain't that something." Her Winchester lowered an inch as emerald patterns danced down the barrel.

For three heartbeats, nobody spoke. Nobody breathed. The ghost-lights hummed a tune that vibrated molars and made rifle sights gleam unnatural green.

Then a Thompson man retched into the scrub oak.

The spell broke.

Ethan's boot scuffed the map. "We move at dawn." His gaze locked with Thompson's. No room for debate.

Jasper recovered first, smoothing his waistcoat. "Typical. Big brother always -"

Deke spat at his feet. The wad of tobacco hit the glowing fog and sizzled. "Finish that sentence. I dare you."

But the cold fire above them dimmed as suddenly as it appeared. Normal stars emerged like hesitant spectators. Somewhere in the dark, water chuckled over stones.

Clara sniffed. "Smells like burnt sage now. Or maybe that's just Thompson's bullshit cooking off."

Lily crouched, pressing a palm to damp earth. When she stood, crushed yarrow petals drifted from her fingers. "The Breath favors no man's schedule."

Thompson opened his mouth, but Ethan was already rolling the map. "We'll take the east fork." The words hung in the air, sharp as trap springs.

Overhead, the last luminous tendrils dissolved into nothing.

***

The jade burned against Lily's collarbone like a struck match.

She didn't flinch. Just pressed two fingers to the carved herbs on the pendant's face—*huang qin, dang gui*, their ancient contours humming under her touch. Above them, the last wisps of Valley's Breath dissolved into ordinary starlight, leaving the smell of ozone and something faintly herbal clinging to the rocks.

"East fork's suicide," Deke growled, not looking at Jasper. His knuckles whitened around his rifle stock. "Three confirmed rock slides this season. No water sources marked past—"

"Marked by who?" Lily interrupted. The pendant's heat spread through her ribs, steady as a heartbeat. She kicked a tuft of sagebrush. Brittle roots snapped, revealing soil the color of crushed hematite. "Map says barren. But this?" She crumbled earth between her fingers. "Five years since last burn. Silverleaf phacelia sprouting here—see the hairs?"

Henry Thompson chuckled, the sound too smooth for canyon country. "Botany lessons are charming, Miss Chen, but my men have Winchesters and dynamite. Your little weeds won't stop cougars." He stepped closer to Ethan, boots crunching dead man's fingers blooms. "Blake. Be reasonable. Combine our supplies, we clear either path by noon."

Lily's pendant flared.

She spun toward the eastern trail before realizing she'd moved. A jackrabbit bolted through rabbitbrush, its path etching a jagged line toward shadowed cliffs. Her grandmother's voice coiled through memory —*When the land speaks, child, you sprint first and apologize later.*

Ethan studied the rabbit's wake. "Dynamite brings attention."

"Attention?" Henry's grin showed molars. "From what? Prairie dogs?"

Clara spat. "From things making those." She jerked her chin skyward where phantom lights had danced minutes before. Her thumb rubbed the Winchester's receiver—three notches filed deep.

Jasper materialized at Deke's flank like smoke. "Still jumping at shadows, big brother?" His breath carried whiskey and anise. "Remember that cellar in El Paso? You screamed like a—"

Deke's elbow connected with Jasper's solar plexus. A wet *oof* cut through canyon silence.

Nobody drew iron.

"Enough." Ethan didn't raise his voice. Didn't need to. The word landed like a coffin lid.

Lily watched a yucca stalk tremble fifty yards east. No wind stirred the valley. Her pendant cooled abruptly—decision made. She turned to Henry. "Your boots."

"Excuse me?"

"Custom-made. Calfskin. Worth three months' Army pay." She nodded at crimson stains marring the toes. "But you walked through woolly ragwort back there. Sap eats leather." She smiled sweetly. "Better hurry west. Save the shoes."

Clara snorted. Thompson's men exchanged glances. One sniffed his own bootheel.

Henry's jovial mask cracked. Just for a heartbeat—a twitch under his left eye, fingers curling like talons. Then the grin returned, colder. "Charming." He turned to Ethan. "Last offer."

Ethan scuffed his boot through Lily's phacelia patch. Purple petals clung to his soles. "We'll manage."

Jasper laughed, rubbing his bruised gut. "Christ, Blake. Leading lambs to slaughter now?" His gaze locked with Deke's. "Should've stayed in Boston, big brother. Might've kept your hands clean this time."

Deke's trigger finger spasmed.

Lily saw it first—the fractional dip of his right shoulder, the shift from posturing to killing stance. She stepped between the brothers, her back to Jasper. "Deke." She gripped his forearm, feeling corded muscle tremble. "The phacelia."

"What about the damn weed?"

"Its roots prevent infection." She pressed harder. "When brewed with mullein."

A beat. Two. Deke exhaled through his nose. "That a fact."

"Mm." She didn't let go. "Also repels scorpions."

Clara sauntered over, Winchester propped on her hip. "Hate scorpions. Nasty little bastards." She glared at Jasper. "Sting you when you're not looking."

Henry adjusted his cravat with jerky motions. "Enjoy your scenic route." He wheeled toward the western trail, snapping fingers. "Move out!"

Thompson's men scrambled. All except Jasper.

"This ain't over, Deacon," he murmured, using the name only family knew.

Deke froze.

Jasper smirked. "Ma cried herself blind, you know. After you ran."

The canyon held its breath.

Lily's hand slid to her pendant. Warm again. Not warning—urging.

"Sounded like rain," Deke said suddenly.

"What?"

"Her crying." He spat near Jasper's polished boots. "Always thought it sounded like spring rain on our old porch roof." His eyes were flint. "Tell me, little brother—she ever weep for you?"

Jasper's cheek twitched.

Clara racked her Winchester. The *kachunk* echoed off sandstone. "Y'all gonna court, or we walking?"

Ethan shouldered his pack. "East."

They left Jasper standing in yarrow and silence.

Lily waited until the others were twenty paces ahead before pausing. She snapped off a woolly ragwort stem, its oozing sap coating her fingers. Quick hands smeared the yellow goo across their backtrail— crude X's on juniper trunks.

"Won't stop trackers," Deke muttered, appearing beside her.

"No." She wiped sap-streaked hands on her trousers. "But poison ivy looks similar from saddle height."

He stared at her.

She shrugged. "Land provides."

Ahead, Clara crowed laughter at something Ethan said. The sound bounced off cliff walls, defiant as a hawk's cry.

Deke fell into step beside Lily. "That phacelia crap. Really fight infection?"

"If prepared properly."

"And the scorpion thing?"

"Total horseshit."

His snort was almost a laugh. Almost.

The eastern cliffs loomed, bleeding long shadows across their path. Lily's pendant pulsed once—approval or warning, she couldn't tell.

Didn't matter. They'd chosen.

Somewhere behind them, a Thompson man started swearing about itching ankles.

***

The eastern trail chewed boot leather like tobacco spit. Ethan adjusted his pack straps, canvas biting shoulders still sore from last week's hailstorm. Above them, the Valley's Breath swirled—greenish wisps darting between juniper branches like drunken fireflies.

"Tighter'n a tick's ass in there." Clara jerked her chin at the narrowing canyon ahead, thumb brushing Winchester iron. Her grin showed too many teeth. "Bet my left tit we find cougar dens."

Deke spat near her boot. "Bet your right one we find Thompson's boys 'fore sunset." His fingers kept drifting toward the bowie knife sheathed at his lower back, leather grip worn smooth from similar gestures.

Lily crouched by a seep spring, mud squelching between her fingers. "Phacelia," she announced, smearing purple blooms across a fresh scrape on her forearm. The jade pendant swung loose from her neck, catching spectral light. "Also rattlesnake weed. Also poison sumac."

"Helpful hierarchy," Ethan muttered, unfolding his mother's map against a lichen-crusted boulder. The parchment rippled as though breathing—same way it had in his childhood bedroom during thunderstorms. He pressed Blake surveying weights (twin obsidian stones from Crow territory) against curling corners.

Aiyana appeared soundlessly, her braid beads whispering. She traced a route through the canyon's maze with calloused fingers. "Third fork west leads to deadfall. Fifth east to quicksand springs." Her nail split the difference. "Middle path holds hunger."

Clara snorted. "We brought bacon."

"And cliff faces hold patience," Aiyana countered. Her gaze lingered on the pendant's glow reflected in Lily's sweat-damp collar. "The Breath favors bold steps. Not careless ones."

Deke's chuckle held no humor. He hefted his Sharps rifle, barrel sweeping across distant scree slopes. "Bold gets you ventilated. Careless gets you buried." The weapon paused mid-swing. "Movement. Eleven o'clock. Coyote or fool?"

Ethan squinted where sunlight fractured through quartz veins. "Fool coyote, maybe." He rolled the map with military precision, tucking it into an oilskin sleeve. "We'll take the middle hunger path. Double-time before those clouds—" he jabbed at anvils massing behind Sentinel Peak "—start pissing arrows."

The company shouldered burdens in practiced silence. Lily scattered crushed yarrow behind them. Clara hummed "Sweet Betsy from Pike" off-key. Deke kept his Sharps' hammer at half-cock, eyes scanning every shadow-kissed crevice.

As they entered the canyon's jagged maw, the Valley's Breath intensified. Emerald tendrils licked stone walls, illuminating handholds in the gathering dark. The air tasted of burnt sage and impending rain. Somewhere above, iron rang on flint—real or memory, none could say.

Ethan's compass needle spun lazily in its brass housing. He snapped the lid shut. "Pace count," he ordered, pulling a knotted cord from his pocket. Each bead represented sixty-two soldier strides. The others fell into line—Clara's mocking salute, Deke's protective rearguard pivot, Lily's herb-stained fingers brushing guardian X's on stone.

Aiyana brought up the rear, her braids now threaded with fresh juniper sprigs. When the first fat raindrops struck sandstone, she didn't flinch. When the spectral lights winked out abruptly, she simply lit a pitch-pine torch. Its flame danced across thousand-year-old petroglyphs of spirals and stags.

No one remarked when the canyon walls began humming. No one panicked when Deke's canteen started weeping rust-colored liquid. They walked as the valley demanded—backs bent but unbowed, packs lighter only in metaphor, choices etched deeper than the map's fragile ink.

Somewhere beyond the storm's curtain, Henry Thompson's men would be rubbing poison ivy rashes and cursing Chen family tricks. Somewhere behind thunderheads, Jasper O'Sullivan was likely counting bullets. Ahead lay only the next step, and the next, and the next—their footfalls swallowed by living stone.

CHAPTER 9

Secrets Unearthed

THE VALLEY'S BREATH COILED overhead like phosphorescent serpents, throwing fractured light across the split in the trail. Ethan spat a pine needle from his mouth and thumbed the Blake Wayfinder compass hanging open in his palm. Its needle spun twice before locking on the left-hand path where the ghost-lights writhed thickest.

"Left," he said, snapping the brass case shut.

Henry Thompson's boot scuffed dirt behind him. "That's three times now you've ignored the mapped routes." The cartographer's voice carried the clipped precision of a man choking back fury. "Those journals of yours aren't gospel, Blake."

Ethan didn't turn. He was already moving, the leather satchel containing his mother's journals slapping against his hip. "Map says there's a sheer cliff here. You seeing any cliffs?"

What they found instead were sandstone teeth gnashing upwards through the earth. Lily Chen flowed through the obstacle course of razor-edged boulders like water through canyon cracks, her fingers brushing leaves and bark as she passed.

"Devil's club here," she announced, not breaking stride. A thorn-studded plant quivered where she'd marked it with a strip of red cloth from her pack. "Touch it and you'll piss pus for a week."

Deke snorted somewhere in the rear. "Charming."

They climbed. The air turned to soup - hot, thick, stinking of resin and stone. Ethan's shirt clung to his spine as Lily's voice cut through the rasp of labored breathing:

"Yarrow cluster. Somebody step on it if you want bleeding stopped later."

Henry's map case clattered against rock. "Could we perhaps focus less on weeds and more on not dying of exposure?"

Lily crouched by a spray of white flowers, her jade pendant swinging free. "Your choice, Eastern boy. Tourniquet or cauterization when your fancy boots shred your ankles." She pocketed a handful of blooms. "Both hurt like hell."

Ethan hid a grin against his canteen.

By midday, even the pack mules had tongues lolling. They collapsed in the skeletal shade of lightning-struck pines, Lily spreading her harvest across a sun-bleached bandana.

"Chew this," she ordered, tossing Deke a wrinkled root. "Tastes like Satan's asshole but keeps the thirst manageable."

Clara prodded a spiky leaf bundle. "And these?"

"Prickly pear pads. Burn the spines off, eat them when the whiskey runs out." Lily's knife flashed, sectioning a gnarled tuber. "This one's death camas. Looks like onion. Kills slower than arsenic."

Ethan watched her fingers work - precise, unhesitating. "Where'd you learn all this?"

"My grandmother's cure for my first heartbreak involved a shovel and an acre of Jerusalem artichokes." Lily didn't look up. "You apprentice quick under Chinese matriarchs."

Deke spit out his root. "Christ almighty! Told you it tastes evil."

"Swallow anyway." Lily tossed him another. "Unless you prefer hallucinating from dehydration like those Legion idiots in your mother's journals."

Ethan stiffened. "You read them?"

"Smelled the wolf willow infusion pages from across camp last night." Her eyes finally met his, dark and unreadable. "Your mother wasn't just recording history. She was brewing storm warnings."

The rock beneath Ethan suddenly felt hotter. Before he could respond, Clara's shout sliced through the air:

"Scorpion! Big bastard in the bedroll!"

Chaos erupted. Ethan lunged for his rifle. Lily moved faster, slapping a leather glove over the thriving fabric.

"Idiot!" She shook the stunned arachnid into a glass jar. "Striped tail means it's shy. Red claw? You'd be dead before sunrise." Her glare swept the group. "Check your gear twice. This isn't Philadelphia garden party country."

When the commotion died, Ethan found himself shoulder-to-shoulder with Lily at the cliff's crumbling edge. Below them, the valley unfolded like a rumpled quilt stitched with pine and sorrow.

"Your mother's notes on the Legion's last stand..." Lily spoke to the horizon. "They didn't starve. Didn't thirst." Her jade pendant caught the light as she turned. "Pages reek of monkshood and nightshade. Poisons, Blake."

Ethan's thumb worried the compass' engravings. "You saying they ate toxic plants?"

"I'm saying someone made sure they did." Wind whipped loose strands of hair across her face. "Five trained soldiers don't mistake death camas for wild onions. Not unless..."

A shale slide clattered below. Ethan's hand closed around her elbow, pulling her back from the edge. Her skin burned through the linen sleeve.

"Not unless forced," he finished.

Lily didn't shake free. "Your compass pointed true today. Tomorrow..." She nodded at the Valley's Breath now coiling eastward. "Spirits change their minds faster than river currents."

Somewhere behind them, Deke cursed at a stubborn mule. Lily's elbow slipped from Ethan's grip as she moved toward the chaos, leaving the scent of crushed sage in her wake.

Ethan stared at the compass. Its needle trembled, no longer pointing left or right, but straight down into the hungry earth.

***

The rifle shot cracked twice - Deke's signal. Ethan's hand went to his Colt before he registered the pattern. *Found something. Come quick.*

Lily's eyebrow arched. "Your tracker's got timing like a bad comedian." She rubbed the spot on her elbow where his fingers had dug in moments before.

They found Deke knee-deep in nightmare trees. The pines here grew sideways, trunks twisted like broken fingers clawing at granite sky. No birdsong. No wind. Just the creak of arthritic branches and the sour tang of old violence seeping from the ground.

"Camp," Deke grunted, kicking a rusted tin plate fused to the forest floor. "Military issue. 1873 stamp." His boot nudged a moss-eaten boot heel still laced around ankle bones gone chalky white. "Five sets of remains. Maybe six."

Ethan crouched, brushing dirt from a tarnished belt buckle. The embossed eagle stared blindly upward, wings spread in perpetual flight. His mother's journal entry flared behind his eyes - *Legion's final muster roll: 6 souls*. The compass in his pocket grew heavy.

"Christ alive," Henry muttered, poking a skeleton's ribcage with his walking stick. "Looks like they tried building a firepit." The blackened stones formed a perfect circle, untouched by forty years of storms. Ash still clung to the central depression like gunpowder residue.

Lily knelt beside a shattered medicine bottle, gloved fingers sifting through blue glass shards. "Strychnine residue." She held a fragment to the muted light. "Military doctors carried this for mercy doses. Last resort."

Deke's find made them all go quiet - a Colt Army revolver wedged in a tree knot, barrel split like peeled bark. Three cartridges remained in the cylinder. Fired. Unfired. Fired.

"Madness," Clara breathed, tracing the claw marks raked across the pistol grip. "Whatever chased them didn't use bullets."

Ethan's thumbs worked instinctively, aligning artifacts with sketches from his mother's journals. The coded symbols matched perfectly - a tattered map fragment wrapped around a dried tobacco pouch. His gut tightened as overlapping circles and angular glyphs resolved into familiar patterns. *Blake family cipher. Mother's handwriting in the margins.*

"Got something." The words tasted like copper. Three pairs of boots circled him.

Lily's shadow fell across the parchment. "That's no supply list."

"Coordinates. Dates. And... directions for evading pursuit." Ethan's knife tip traced the largest symbol - an eye weeping three tears. "They weren't lost. They were *herded*."

Henry laughed sharp enough to startle a jay from its roost. "Herded? By what? Ghosts and fairy tales?"

"By men." Deke spat a stream of tobacco juice that sizzled against cold iron. "Men leave tracks. Men bleed." He jerked his chin at the ruined pistol. "Men don't make seasoned soldiers chew their own guns."

The Valley's Breath chose that moment to coil through the clearing - not fog, but something older. It pooled around their ankles, whispering against rusted spurs and sun-bleached buttons. Lily's jade pendant glowed faintly, casting sickly light on the map's key phrase:

THEY COME WHEN THE STARS BLINK OUT.

Clara crossed herself. Henry adjusted his spectacles three times in quick succession. Deke just stared at the skeletal hand still gripping a rusted canteen, thumb joint wedged stubbornly against the cap.

"Forty years," Ethan said quietly. "Whatever happened here..." He folded the map into his breast pocket, feeling the weight of six graves pressing against his ribs. "...it's not finished."

Above them, the twisted pines creaked in agreement.

***

Clara's bootheel ground a rusted spur into the dirt as she kicked through the debris. The others clustered around Ethan like chicks to a hen, jabbering about star patterns and troop movements. A cracked leather satchel slumped against a lightning-blasted pine caught her eye - the kind old Doc Henderson back home used to carry his tonics in.

She crouchedd, fingers brushing mildew-soft leather. The rotted strap disintegrated, spilling contents that clinked like dead men's teeth. A tarnished spoon. Shards of blue ceramic. And there, glinting dully beneath a scrap of oilcloth...

"The hell you doing over here, Princess?" Deke materialized from the twisted pines, thumbs hooked in his gunbelt. "Eyes up. This ain't no..."

The words died as Clara's hand closed around cold silver. The locket's hinge screamed when she pried it open. Two faces stared back from a daguerreotype smaller than a postage stamp - a young cavalry lieutenant and his bride. Her knuckles went bone-white around the keepsake.

"Granddad?" The whisper slipped out before she could bite it off.

Deke's shadow fell across the photograph. "That's your blood in this shithole?"

The clearing snapped into razor focus. Lily paused mid-sentence by the campfire pit, a brittle leaf crumbling between her fingers. Henry adjusted his spectacles so hard the wire frames dug grooves in his nose. Only Ethan kept methodically cataloging artifacts, though his shoulders stiffened beneath his trail-worn coat.

Clara surged upright, the locket chain biting into her palm. "Says 'To J.B. - Against All Storms' inside. My granddaddy's initials. His..." She swallowed the word 'funeral' along with a sudden bile taste. They'd buried an empty coffin draped in regimental colors while she threw roses and lies at weeping relatives.

Lily appeared beside her smelling of crushed yarrow and concern. "This J.B. served with the Legion?"

"Deserted." The truth tore free like a bullet. "Winter of '79. Military police came asking after..." She turned the locket over, revealing engraving only family would know - the crude horse head Pa had etched during his drinking days. "Never said why he ran. Ma claimed honor. I called bullshit."

Henry cleared his throat. "Fascinating! Perhaps your ancestor left journals? Letters?"

"For a man who talks plenty, you sure swallow stupid whole." Deke spat near Henry's boots. "Girl's kin turns tail, ends up here?" He jerked his chin at the skeletal hand still clutching a rusted canteen. "That reeks worse than week-old buffalo guts."

Ethan's map case snapped shut. "We don't know what happened here."

"We know Clara's been itching since Whiterock to cut northwest," Deke countered. "Same direction those lunatics were running."

The accusation hung like gunsmoke. Clara met Ethan's gaze across the corpse of a campfire older than her pa. Let him see the truth she'd just now realized herself - every story about her grandfather's heroics stank of cheap perfume on a three-dollar whore.

"Found this sewn into my swaddle." She flipped the locket at Ethan. It arced silver in the fading light. "Ma said it proved our line ran brave. You know what I see now? A man who abandoned his unit. Left his wife. Hid like a..."

"Rabbit?" Lily suggested softly.

"Damn straight." Clara's laugh came out jagged. "Guess the apple didn't fall far, huh? Always chasing..." She kicked the satchel, sending a corroded harmonica skittering against a rock. "...whatever the fuck this is."

Ethan studied the locket's inscription. "Your grandfather's choices don't dictate yours."

"Don't they?" Deke's hand rested on his Colt. "Girl's got red in her ledger now. You trust her compass?"

Lily stepped between them, jade pendant flashing. "We trusted yours after the Bear Creek ambush."

"That was different!"

"How? Because she's a woman? Or because her ghost might actually matter?"

The wind chose that moment to riffle through the twisted pines. Dozens of rusted canteens dangling from branches like macabre wind chimes clanked a discordant tune. Henry yelped when a desiccated owl carcass plopped into the ashes at his feet.

Ethan palmed the locket. "We move northeast at dawn."

"Bullshit!" Clara and Deke said in unison.

He ignored them, addressing the rotting satchel instead. "Legion remnants all face northwest. Whatever they fled from..." His calloused thumb brushed the locket's engraved horse. "...they died facing it. That's where answers lie."

Lily nodded toward the gathering gloom. "The Valley's Breath stirs earlier each night. Whatever path we take..."

"Gets taken quick," Deke finished grimly.

Clara stared at the skeletal hand. Three fingers missing - frostbite, if the stories held. Granddad J.B. had all digits when they buried that empty box. She waited for grief. For shame. All that came was the marrow-deep certainty she'd been saddling the wrong ghosts her whole damn life.

"Northwest then." She snatched the locket back, chain snapping taut. "Let's see what scared the piss out of Grandpa."

Deke spat. Henry mumbled equations. Lily pressed a sprig of purple sage into Clara's palm - for courage or masking rot, it hardly mattered.

As they broke camp, Clara watched Ethan pocket a rusted dog tag stamped J.B. Bennett. The lie settled between them like cocked iron. She'd known the second she saw that locket.

Her grandfather never made it out of this valley alive.

***

The campfire popped, sending embers skittering across Clara's boot. She ground the sparks dead under her heel, watching Ethan trace the etched letters on that damn dog tag. J.B. Bennett. Same initials stamped on her mother's wedding chest back home. Same lies carved in granite over an empty grave.

"Moonrise in twenty." Deke lobbed a charred stick into the flames. "Either we move now or play sitting ducks for whatever spooked the Legion."

Henry's pencil scratched frantic circles in his journal. "Without proper azimuth calculations—"

"Azimuth my ass." Clara flicked a pinecone at the scholar's knee. "You want numbers? Three generations of Bennetts thought Grandpa died building the Northern Pacific. Turns out he was busy getting massacred here. That math add up for you?"

Lily's mortar clinked as she ground another batch of that bitter-smelling salve. "Family ghosts make poor trailmates."

Ethan stood suddenly, the dog tag clenched in his fist. Firelight carved shadows under his cheekbones. "We press northwest at first light."

Deke spat. "Your funeral."

"Actually," Clara drawled, spinning her grandfather's locket on its broken chain, "seems it's mine."

The pause stretched taut. Somewhere beyond the fire's reach, the Valley's Breath coiled between the pines—pale tendrils testing their defenses.

Lily stood, wiping her hands on faded trousers. "The Legion's pursuers likely knew these woods better than we do. Traveling by day won't save us from—"

"Old bones and older fears," Ethan cut in. His eyes met Clara's, steady as a gunsight. "But fresh lies? Those'll kill faster than any phantom."

Henry snapped his journal shut. "This reeks of emotional compromise!"

"So does your cologne, professor." Clara flipped the locket closed. "But last I checked, stink ain't fatal."

A log collapsed in the fire. Sparks spiraled upward, brief constellations dying in the mist. Ethan knelt, spreading the Legion's tattered map across cold earth. Water stains bloomed like blood across the parchment. "Legion scouts marked seven waypoints before they..." His thumb hovered over a charcoal slash. "...stopped making entries."

Deke leaned in, squinting. "That's Smuggler's Notch."

"Was." Lily's finger brushed the edge of a teastain. "Two landslides since. Pass is walled off."

Clara crouched opposite Ethan. "Granddad's last letter mentioned a shortcut. Cut through Dead Man's Gulch, ride the shale slides down."

Deke barked a laugh. "Shale slides eat horses whole."

"Funny." Clara bared teeth. "That's exactly how J.B.'s obituary said he died."

The admission hung sharp as a skinning knife. Lily stopped grinding herbs. Henry's spectacles slipped down his nose.

Ethal rose, the map crackling in his grip. "We'll scout the gulch at dawn. Clara takes point on route selection."

Deke's coffee tin hit dirt. "The hell she does!"

"You question my lead?" Ethan's voice stayed soft. Deadly soft.

"I question her spine when we find granddaddy's corpse mid-chew!"

Clara lunged. Lily caught her arm, calloused palm pressing the old cavalry locket into flesh. "Easy, hellcat. He wants you unsteady."

Ethan stepped between Deke and Clara, a living wall. "We clear the gulch by noon or double back. Majority rules after that."

"Majority." Deke spat the word like phlegm. "Buncha greenhorns following a walking guilt trip." He stomped toward the picket line, muttering about sane men and early graves.

Lily pressed a leaf bundle into Henry's shaking hands. "Boil these into tea. Steadies nerves."

The scholar blinked. "What nerve endings remain..."

Clara found Ethan repacking the Legion's artifacts. His hands moved precise—tarnished compasses, moldy diaries, the ruined photograph of some long-dead infantryman's sweetheart. All the broken keepsakes of butchered men.

"You knew." She didn't make it a question.

He didn't look up. "Suspected."

"And the tag?"

Ethan's knuckles whitened around Private Bennett's dented ID. "Proof stays buried till you want it dug."

The mist thickened, dampening voices around the dying fire. Clara watched him stash the relic bag, leadership weighing heavier than any pack. Her laugh came out razor-edged. "Hell of a time to grow a conscience, Blake."

"Conscience?" He shouldered the kit, blue eyes glinting frost in the dark. "Practicality. Secrets fester. Better yours than mine."

She almost admired the bastard's honesty.

By the time the first coyote yipped, they'd doused the flames. The Ghost Walker's Dance swirled ankle-deep now—cold fingers plucking at bootlaces. Clara took first watch, back against a lightning-split pine. Somewhere northwest, under tons of scree and shame, James Bartholomew Bennett moldered.

She spun his locket once, twice, before slipping it down her shirt. Let it burn against breastbone. Proof against future lies.

Ethan's silhouette appeared ridge-top, already scanning tomorrow's path. Always two steps ahead, that one. Clara cocked her Winchester.

Let him plan. Let them all scheme.

Dead men's trails always led somewhere worth bleeding for.

CHAPTER 10

The Hidden Valley

T HE RIDGE BIT INTO Ethan's palms as he hauled himself up the last few feet. Below him, the expedition team froze mid-step – a dozen pairs of boots hovering over crumbling shale. He didn't need to turn around to know Deke already had his Colt halfway out of its holster.

"Hold." Ethan's voice cut through the wind whipping across the plateau. His left eyelid twitched, that old nervous tic flaring as he raised a hand against the glare. The scar along his thumb stretched tight. "You seeing this?"

Lily shoved past a pack mule, field notebook already open. "If you've found another fossil bed, I swear to God, Blake—" The pencil slipped from her fingers. It rolled toward the precipice, disappearing into swirling mists that coiled like living smoke below their boots.

The valley unfolded like a drunkard's treasure map – all jagged canyons bleeding into meadows where plants pulsed with faint bioluminescence. A river cut through the basin, its water the unnatural blue of apothecary bottles. Somewhere below, something that looked suspiciously like a redwood swayed despite the still air.

Deke spat a stream of tobacco juice that arced over the cliff. "Place stinks like a whorehouse perfumery."

"That's *Osmorhiza aristata* mixed with... Christ, is that *Datura wrightii?*" Lily's fingers twitched toward her specimen jars. "The pigmentation anomalies alone could—"

"Save the botany lesson." Ethan crouched, pebbles skittering under his boots. His father's journal burned against his ribcage. Page fourteen: *The rocks bleed silver here.* Below them, quartz veins spiderwebbed across granite walls, gleaming wet.

Clara hip-checked a boulder, sending a rockslide cascading into the void. "Hell's bells, who's dick do I gotta suck to get down there?"

The mules brayed. Deke's hand shot out, clamping on Clara's suspenders as she leaned too far. "Try that again, firecracker, you'll be sucking Satan's by sundown."

Ethan ignored them, tracing the cliff face with narrowed eyes. "Switchbacks. There, through the mist."

"Or we could slide." Clara jammed her boot into a scree slope. Gravel exploded downward. Somewhere in the valley, unseen birds shrieked metallic cries.

Lily palmed a brass locket watch. "Two hours until full dark. If we want to—"

"We're going." Ethan shrugged off his pack, rope already uncoiling in his hands. "Deke, take rear guard. Clara, stop trying to kill yourself. Doc —try not to lick anything venomous."

The descent turned into a shit-show by the third switchback. Lily's petticoats snagged on manzanita thorns. Clara's "shortcut" nearly brained the lead mule. Deke moved like a shadow, fingers brushing every other rock—testing, always testing.

Halfway down, the air turned syrupy. Ethan's collar clung to his neck. That sweet reek Deke had noticed now seeped into their pores— honeysuckle dipped in kerosene.

"Hold up." Deke's boot nudged a skeletal pinecone the size of a wagon wheel. "That ain't right."

Lily practically vibrated. "*Pinus longaeva,* but the scale suggests—"

Gunmetal clicked. Every head swiveled toward Deke's drawn revolver. "Movement. Two o'clock."

The valley floor rippled. What they'd taken for shrubs unfurled violet tendrils toward the fading light. A stand of willows rattled bone-white leaves.

Clara whooped. The sound caromed off canyon walls, multiplying into a ghostly chorus.

"You happy now?" Deke growled as the last echo died.

Ethan wiped sweat from his Remington's grip. "Let's find out."

***

The valley floor swallowed them whole. Ethan's boots sank into moss that pulsed faintly blue with each step. Clara kicked at a cluster of seed pods that chimed like sleigh bells. "Well ain't this dandy," she muttered, reloading her Winchester with hands still shaking from the descent.

Shadows shifted.

Deke's knife cleared its sheath before the rest of them blinked. Three hooded figures melted from the trembling undergrowth, obsidian-tipped spears catching the strange light.

"Easy." Ethan spread empty palms, thumb brushing the Blake family crest etched into his mother's compass. The central figure stepped forward, lowering her hood to reveal salt-and-pepper braids threaded with crow feathers.

"You're tracking silt from Deadman's Gulch in my clean riverbed," Aiyana Whitefeather said by way of greeting. Her buckskin tunic showed intricate quillwork patterns Ethan vaguely recognized from his mother's journals - half-finished sketches labeled *Legion sigils?* in Sarah Blake's cramped handwriting.

Lily surged forward, jade pendant swinging. "Your valley's ecosystem exhibits symbiotic relationships I've only read about in—"

Aiyana's raised finger froze the botanist mid-sentence. "Dr. Chen. Your great-grandmother wrote the treatise on ghostroot cultivation. We still use her grafting techniques." She turned to Ethan, dark eyes sharp as flint. "And Mr. Blake. The man who digs up his mother's ghosts."

The compass bit into Ethan's palm. "My father—"

"—rode with Colonel Hargrave's doomed company. Yes." Aiyana snapped her fingers. One of her sentries produced a rust-caked canteen bearing the Legion's winged serpent emblem. "We pulled six survivors from the snows in '62. Your father wasn't among them."

Clara spat tobacco juice near Aiyana's moccasin. "This a history lesson or a shakedown?"

The Guardian didn't blink. "Your explosives expert. How many mountains has she peeled open this year?"

Ethan's crew shifted uneasily. Lily's fingers twitched toward a pulsating mushroom cap. Deke kept three separate exits in his sightlines.

"Enough." Aiyana's cloak swirled as she turned, revealing a hide satchel stitched with Legion symbols intertwined with Blackfoot motifs. "Walk. Breathe. See what your greed would destroy."

The village unfolded like one of Lily's specimen drawings - meticulous and impossibly alive. Houses shaped from living trees curved around thermal springs. Children scaled vine lattices bearing melons bigger than their heads. An old man whistled, sending a ripple through barley fields that parted like obedient dogs.

"Survivors rebuilt with our ancestors," Aiyana said as they passed a forge hammering metal Ethan didn't recognize - lighter than steel, glowing faintly green. "Your father's company stole Shoshone horses. Murdered Pawnee scouts. Yet when winter broke them, we offered shelter."

Ethan stopped cold beside a communal well. Carved into its stone lip: William Blake, 1862. His thumbnail found the matching groove in his compass lid.

"Bullshit," Clara hissed. "Nobody winters here without—"

Aiyana snapped a yellow bloom from its stalk. Frost crystals immediately feathered across the petals. "Our first lesson in valley hospitality: never question the gardener."

Lily made a choked noise, fingers hovering over the freezing flower. "This...this shouldn't be possible. Hybridization requires generations of —"

"You'll find eighteen varieties of wheat developed since your last agricultural survey," Aiyana said, plucking a golden stalk. "Try stealing these patents, Miss Langston."

Ethan barely heard them. The well's carvings blurred beneath his calloused fingers - same angular script from his mother's journals, same dates as her unexplained month-long "survey trips." His chest tightened like the day he'd found Sarah's bloodstained maps.

Deke materialized at his shoulder. "They got you square in the crosshairs, boss." He nodded toward children playing with bowstrings that hummed when drawn. "Place is armed to the teeth."

Aiyana appeared between two hanging gourds without disturbing a single vine. "Your hired gun's right. We protect our own." She pressed something cold into Ethan's hand - his father's cavalry ring, etched with the Legion motto: *Ad Astra Per Aspera*.

The ground tilted. Ethan saw his mother burning letters in their Franklin stove, heard her whiskey-rough laugh. *You want frontier fairy tales? Go dig up your damn fool father.*

"Survivors kept records." Aiyana's voice softened. "William tried leaving three times. Always came back when the passes iced over."

Lily appeared clutching a leaf that shimmered between gold and green. "Their agricultural yield could revolutionize—"

"No." Ethan's fist closed around the ring's jagged edges. "You don't bring railroads to Eden."

Clara barked a laugh. "Since when you get religion?"

He met Aiyana's gaze over the dying frost bloom. Saw his mother's relentless pragmatism twisted into something that could nurture instead of conquer. "We restock. Leave at first light."

The Guardian smiled for the first time - all challenge. "Took your father six weeks to say that." She nodded toward a longhouse smelling of smoked venison. "Eat. Tomorrow's trouble comes soon enough."

Deke fell into step beside Ethan, thumb testing his knife edge. "She's playing you."

"Yeah." Ethan watched Lily crouch to examine bioluminescent tree roots, her pendant casting jade patterns on the bark. "But which one of us?"

Somewhere beyond the ridge, thunder growled. Not the sky.

***

The valley's twilight hummed with insects that glowed like embers. Ethan leaned against a tree whose bark pulsed faintly, watching Clara haggle with a leatherworker over mule feed. Her laugh cut through the dusk – too sharp, too hungry.

"They're already pricing the lumber," Deke muttered, whittling a stick into something dangerous. His boot tapped rhythm against a root that leaked blue sap. "Your call, boss."

Ethan's thumb found the crack in his father's ring. Across the clearing, Lily crouched by a shrub whose leaves rippled from crimson to black. Her pendant swung forward, green light bleeding into the plant's veins. The thing recoiled.

"Christ." Clara materialized beside him reeking of corn whiskey. "You seen their irrigation? Ten years of drought back home, and these savages got streams running uphill." She spat a sunflower seed hull that sizzled where it hit the moss.

Deke's knife stilled. "Word gets out, this place becomes a damn mining camp by solstice."

Lily stood abruptly, wiping soil-streaked hands on her trousers. The motion sent shadows dancing across medicinal carvings on her pendant.

"These biosystems are *anatomically impossible*," she said to nobody, voice trembling with scientific fury. "No recorded pollination vectors, yet the fruiting bodies—"

"Got your miracle cure yet?" Clara drawled.

A leaf detached itself from Lily's sleeve, curling into ash before it hit the ground.

Ethan pushed off the tree. "We're guests here."

"Guests starve," Clara shot back. "My boys in Tombstone ain't getting younger."

The argument dissolved when three valley children scampered past clutching frog-like creatures that sang in minor keys. Deke tracked them until they vanished into a dwelling shaped like an inverted swallow's nest. "Tribe's got no sentries," he murmured. "No stockpiles. You'd think they invented peace."

"Or never had a Carlson among them," Ethan said.

Clara snorted. "I'll take my chances with Carlsons over whatever voodoo makes *that*." She jabbed her chin at a tree whose branches writhed slowly overhead, bulbs bursting into momentary flames that left no smoke.

Lily appeared beside them clutching a hand lens. "The chloroplasts are aligned in tetrahedral patterns. If I could just—"

"No samples," Ethan said.

Her jaw clenched. "My brother—"

"Will still be dying tomorrow." He caught her wrist, felt the rabbit-quick pulse beneath jade-warmed skin. "These people survived the Legion. Think they can't spot a thief?"

Deke chuckled darkly. "Oh, they'll spot her. Question is what they'll do about it."

Firelight bloomed ahead as villagers lit a pyre of fragrant wood. Aiyana stood silhouetted against the flames, braided hair threaded with what looked like living fireflies. Her gaze locked on Ethan's – challenging, patient, older than the redwoods.

Clara elbowed him. "Bet she knows where the gold's buried."

"Bet she'd feed you to those goddamn singing frogs," Deke said.

They settled on log benches that shifted subtly to accommodate weight. Ethan sat apart, back to stone warmed by day's heat. Lily fidgeted with her pendant's silk cord until the braid unraveled.

A youth offered clay cups of something that smoked. Deke sniffed his drink and promptly dumped it in a pitcher plant. The vegetation recoiled, tendrils blackening.

"Real subtle," Clara said.

"Still breathing, ain't I?"

Lily ignored her cup, scribbling in a field notebook. "The rhizomes here exhibit phototropic memory. Imagine applying this to crop rotations —"

"Stop." Ethan's voice carried over the crackling flames.

She looked up, lens flashing. "You don't own discovery."

"Neither do you."

The fire popped, sending up sparks that hovered like accusation. Somewhere in the dark, bioluminescent wolves began to howl.

Deke tested his knife edge against a bench leg. The wood bled resin that smelled of gunpowder. "Guardian's been gone twenty minutes. Your play, Blake."

Clara leaned forward. "We could map the east ridge tonight. Be gone by moonset."

Lily's pencil snapped. "Destroying this place won't absolve your father."

Ethan stood abruptly. The fire dimmed as he passed, embers dying mid-air. He found Aiyana by a waterfall that fell upward into the cliffside.

"You smell like crossroads," she said without turning.

"My men want to pillage. My botanist wants to dissect. What's left for me?"

She cupped water that flowed over her fingers like mercury. "Your father asked the same. Then he learned our trees grow faster when sung to."

"That supposed to mean something?"

"It means William Blake finally understood theft." She opened her hand. The water had crystallized into a perfect cube. "Take nothing, and the valley gives. Take anything..." The cube dissolved into iridescent mist. "Well. You've met our wolves."

Back at the fire, Lily was arguing with a woman whose hair writhed with vine-like growths. "...merely a tissue sample—"

The villager pressed a finger to Lily's pendant. The jade flared, revealing vein-like structures beneath its surface. Both women recoiled.

"*Shèngmìng xiānghù liánjié*," the villager hissed.

Lily stumbled backward. "It... translated that." She clutched the pendant now glowing faintly. "'Life interconnected.'"

Deke materialized behind her. "Pack your kit. We're leaving."

"The hell we are," Clara said.

Ethan watched them all – the war chief's daughter, the mercenary botanist, the killer who smelled ambush in honeysuckle. Beyond the firelight, the luminous forest pulsed like a heartbeat.

"Sunrise," he said. "We vote then."

Clara spat in the fire. It hissed like a sidewinder. "Democracy. How fucking noble."

Later, Ethan found Lily elbow-deep in a compost pit, examining fungi that emitted radio static clicks. Her pendant glowed like swamp gas.

"They're listening," he said.

She didn't look up. "The *Cordyceps ophioglossoides* here could rewrite neurology. Or kill us all."

"Your brother need rewriting or killing?"

Her hands stilled. "I've mapped seventeen species unknown to science. Seventeen *cures*, Ethan."

He knelt, crushing a mushroom underheel. The air filled with the scent of burnt hair. "How many graves you think this valley holds?"

The answer came as wolves began harmonizing in the dark – not howls, but something with chords and intention. A hunting song.

Deke found them there, blade already bloodied. "Clara's missing."

Ethan stared at the dying bioluminescence at their feet. "Then we're already too late."

Somewhere above, thunder cracked – deep and chemical and wrong. The kind that came from cannons, not clouds.

***

The fire popped, sending embers spiraling up toward stars that looked too close. Ethan counted them like bullet holes in a tin can—one for every bad decision that got them here. Aiyana materialized from the dark like smoke given form, braids catching firelight in copper flickers. She didn't ask permission to sit, just settled on a lichen-crusted log that hadn't been there at sundown.

"Your cannons," she said, watching Deke clean his bowie knife with ritual precision. "The thunder-that-isn't. We call them Stone Coughs."

Clara snorted. "Cute. You name your artillery fire?"

"Names give power. My great-grandmother watched soldiers carve through these peaks like rot through fruit." Aiyana scooped dirt, let it sift between her fingers. Glowing mites swarmed the falling grains. "Their blasting powder woke something better left sleeping. Now the mountain spits their own violence back at them, season after season. Poisoned gift."

Lily's thumb worried her jade pendant. "Symbiotic defense mechanism? The valley protects itself through geological memory?"

"Protects. Punishes." Aiyana caught Ethan's gaze. "Depends which side of the dirt you're standing on."

Deke tested his blade's edge against a callus. "Your people ever think about leaving?"

"Every spring when the ghost winds sing." She nodded toward the terraced fields where bioluminescent wheat rippled like liquid mercury. "Then we remember the price of elsewhere."

Clara chucked a pinecone into the flames. "Spare us the folk tales. What's really keeping you prisoner here?"

The log beneath Aiyana sighed, releasing spores that glittered amber in the firelight. Ethan's skin prickled—same way it had when Ma's journals described Legionnaires vanishing into living stone.

"1873," Aiyana said. "Survey team camped where you're sitting. Took samples. Made promises. Ate supper." Her eyes tracked something moving in the dark beyond the fire. "Come dawn, their coffee still steamed in tin cups. Boot prints led straight into limestone walls."

Lily leaned forward. "Petrifaction process? Rapid mineralization through—"

"Consequences." Aiyana stood abruptly, shedding shadows. "You carry your father's compass, Ethan Blake. But direction requires two things—a needle, and the wisdom not to follow it blindly."

The fire snapped loud as a gunshot. When the sparks cleared, she was gone. Deke spat into the flames. "Well that wasn't ominous as shit."

Clara kicked over the log Aiyana had vacated. It crumbled into fingerbone-shaped splinters. "Theatre. Whole damn valley's a medicine show with better props."

Ethan stared at the disturbed earth where Aiyana sat. Tiny mushrooms already pushed through soil, glowing faintly as they formed perfect concentric circles. Patterns within patterns. His gut tightened—same feeling as holding Ma's journal cipher key over Legion maps, watching coordinates align with burial sites.

Lily crouched beside him, pendant casting green light across the fungal growth. "These weren't here ten minutes ago. The mycelium network reacts to—"

"Pack your specimens." Ethan stood, grinding the closest mushroom cluster under his bootheel. The air soured with vinegar stench. "We leave at first light."

Deke's knife stilled. "Thought we were voting."

"Changed the ballot." Ethan watched tendrils of luminous fog coil between trees—Ghost Walker's Dance, Aiyana called it. Warning or welcome, depending who you asked. His father had asked. Then kept digging. "Buried things stay buried for reasons."

Clara laughed—a harsh bark that startled something large into motion through distant brush. "And if the good doctor here objects?" She jerked her chin at Lily, who'd gone statue-still with a fungi sample halfway into her case.

Ethan met Lily's glare. Saw seventeen cures. Seventeen graves. The brother wasting away in some Sanatorium cell. "We're not here to play Messiah. Not even," he added as she opened her mouth, "for family."

The fire chose that moment to collapse in on itself. In the sudden dark, the valley's heartbeat grew louder—not drums, not chants, but the deep thrum of roots moving through stone. Ethan turned his back on it all, Mother's compass cold against his chest. Leadership, he was learning, meant choosing which ghosts to disappoint.

CHAPTER 11

Echoes of Betrayal

CLARA'S BOOTS CARVED TRENCHES in the dirt at the camp's edge, her granddaddy's journal digging into her palm like a branding iron. Moonlight caught the frayed leather binding, the same shade as the old man's tobacco-stained fingers when he'd shoved it at her on his deathbed. *"Prove 'em wrong, girl."* The words curdled in her gut now, sour as three-day milk. Across the firelight, the others moved like shadows—Ethan's broad shoulders hunched over maps, Aiyana's braids swaying as she pointed toward the valley's jagged maw.

"Hell's that s'posed to mean?" Clara muttered, thumbing a page where her granddaddy'd sketched a spiral symbol beside *Cursed Ground, Keep Out.* The ink bled through the paper like poison. Her boot kicked a stone into the dark.

Aiyana's voice carried on the night breeze, crisp as broken glass. "These artifacts aren't trinkets for profit. They're the valley's memory."

Ethan nodded, face all carved marble in the firelight. "Preservation's the priority. We document, we protect." His hand rested on that fancy compass contraption of his, brass gleaming like a dare.

Clara's teeth found the inside of her cheek. *Preservation my ass.* Granddaddy Benson hadn't crawled through Apache territory just to let some academic prisses lock his finds in a glass case. She edged closer, red bandana itching against her neck.

Tommy "Quickshot" Reynolds sprawled against a saddlebag ten paces off, cleaning his Colt with the focus of a surgeon. Moonlight glinted off the barrel as he turned it slowly. "Wouldn't peg you fer the broodin' type, Benson." His chuckle sounded like gravel in a tin can. "Or you plannin' a midnight stroll?"

She froze. "Ain't your concern, Reynolds."

"Concern's free, darlin'. Information costs." His eyes flicked to the journal still clutched in her fist. "That relic's gotta be worth somethin' if you're clutchin' it like last week's wages."

Fire sparked behind Clara's ribs. "It ain't about money."

"Course not." Tommy spun the Colt's cylinder—click, click, click. "But seein' as how our noble leader's set on leavin' every shiny rock untouched..." He jerked his chin toward Ethan and Aiyana, now arguing logistics by the supply crates. "Might be a fella could use a partner. For mutual benefit."

Clara's pulse hammered in her ears. The journal pages crackled as her grip tightened. Granddaddy's looping script blurred: *Proof is in the diggin'.*

"What's your angle, Quickshot?"

Tommy's grin showed too many teeth. "Let's call it... professional curiosity." He rose smooth as smoke, holstering the Colt. "Artifacts're boxed near the draft mules. Guard rotates in twenty."

***

The crates smelled of pine resin and lies. Clara crouched behind a boulder, her lungs burning from the sprint across camp. Two guards flanked the supply area—old Bill chewing tobacco, young Jed staring at the stars like some lovestruck fool. She palmed a pebble, hurled it into the scrub.

Jed stiffened. "Hear that?"

Bill spat brown sludge. "Jackrabbit."

"Sounded bigger."

"Go check then, greenhorn."

Clara pressed flat against cold stone as Jed stumbled past, rifle wavering. Six seconds. Five. She lunged, knees eating dirt as she scrambled behind the nearest crate. Granddaddy's journal jabbed her ribcage.

Top crate. Third layer. Her fingers found rough hemp cord. The knot resisted, sweat making her hands slick. Somewhere behind her, Jed's boots scuffed gravel.

"Ain't nothin' here, Bill!"

"Told ya."

The cord snapped. Clara pried up the lid. Leather-wrapped bundles gleamed dully—stone tools, beadwork, a dagger with turquoise inlay. Granddaddy's sketches come to life. Her throat tightened.

"Lookin' for souvenirs?"

Tommy materialized beside her like a damn specter, thumbs hooked in his belt. Clara nearly headbutted the crate.

"Christ Almighty!"

He crouched, eyeing the loot. "Prettier'n a two-dollar whore." His hand darted out, snagging a carved bone pendant. "Reckon this'd fetch —"

Clara seized his wrist. "We're takin' proof. Not plunder."

Tommy's laugh died as her grip tightened. "Easy, hellcat. Just appraisin'." He pocketed the pendant anyway. "Best hurry. Guard's got the bladder of a field mouse."

Her fingers closed around a obsidian blade wrapped in deerhide— Granddaddy's journal entry #47: *Ceremonial, Blackfoot origin. Proof of settlement.* The leather felt warmer than it should.

Something whistled through the dark.

Tommy yanked her down as an arrow thunked into the crate.

"Well shit," he drawled, drawing iron. "Guess we're popular."

***

The arrow quivered in crate wood like a rattler's warning. Clara's knuckles whitened around the obsidian blade.

"Drop it."

Aiyana's voice cut through the gunpowder haze. Not shouting. Worse —cold clear river water over burning coals. Moonlight caught the silver streaks in her braids as she stepped into view, unarmed, flanked by three warriors with nocked arrows.

Tommy's revolver twitched. "Now darlin', let's not—"

Thwip. An arrow buried itself between his boots. He froze mid-drawl, grin cracking. "Christ's sake, woman!"

The camp erupted—boots pounding gravel, curses in three languages. Ethan emerged shirtless from his bedroll, Blake family revolver gleaming in his fist. Lily materialized behind a whiskey barrel with Deke's Colt Peacemaker trained on Tommy's kneecaps.

Clara's throat burned. "I can explain!"

"You're holding proof!" She brandished Granddaddy's journal, pages flapping like a spooked chicken. "Page forty-seven! *Benson men always document their finds!*" The obsian blade slipped, slicing her palm. Blood pattered on turquoise beads.

Aiyana didn't blink. "Your grandfather stole those during the '68 treaty signing."

The journal turned to lead in Clara's grip. "That's... that ain't..."

Tommy sidestepped his personal arrow. "Hell's bells, it's salvage! Finders keepers!" He flashed that snake-oil smile at Ethan. "C'mon Blake—ain't you always yammerin' 'bout settlin' scores? These trinkets'll fetch enough coin to buy your ma's ghost a damn castle!"

Ethan's hammer cocked. "You're drunker than Custer if you think I'd —"

"*Bullshit!*" Clara's voice cracked. She shook the bloody knife at the gathering crowd. "Y'all been pickin' through my family's legacy since Fort Bridger! What's the difference?!"

"Difference is consent." Aiyana's gaze dropped to the stolen dagger. "And basic respect."

Lily spat tobacco juice near Tommy's boot. "Also we don't piss where we sleep, *tā mā de húndàn.*"

Tommy spread his hands, all mock hurt. "Aw Lil', and here I thought we had somethin' special." His eyes darted to the treeline. "Look, let's vote! Democracy in action! Who wants—"

Ethan's bullet kicked dirt between his feet. "Next one's through your teeth."

For three heartbeats, nobody breathed. Clara watched realization gut Ethan—the slump in his shoulders as Tommy winked. The way his finger trembled ever so slightly on the trigger.

Tommy sniffed. "Well. Ain't this a kick in the—"

Deke's rifle stock caught him mid-sneer. The crack of walnut on jawbone sent Tommy sprawling into the artifact crate. Beads scattered. Arrows tracked his fall.

Clara lunged for the obsidian blade.

Aiyana's moccasin pinned her wrist. "Don't."

The campfire popped. Somewhere, a horse whinnied. Clara stared at the blood pooling under her hand—Granddaddy's ink smearing scarlet across page forty-seven.

Ethan's shadow fell over her. "Why?"

She made the mistake of looking up. His eyes weren't angry. Just... tired. The way Pa's got after the '82 blizzard killed every last steer.

Tommy moaned into the dirt, clutching his face. "Fuck's sake Blake, she's just a kid playin' cowboys an'—"

"Shut up." Ethan didn't raise his voice. Didn't need to. The valley itself seemed to lean closer. "Clara?"

Her tears hit the journal with soft thuds. "He wrote... he said we mattered."

Aiyana knelt, extracting the dagger from numb fingers. "Stealing fire doesn't make you warm." She nodded to her warriors. "Bind them both."

As rawhide cords bit into Clara's wrists, she caught Ethan mouthing something to Lily—three syllables that looked suspiciously like *check the horses*. His mother's compass glinted cold at his belt.

Tommy spat blood and a tooth. "Real classy, Blake. Real goddamn—"

The rifle butt came down again.

Quiet reclaimed the valley.

***

The rifle butt's echo still hung in the air when Deke's boot nudged Tommy's ribs. "Try spittin' again," he growled, thumb brushing the bone handle of his skinning knife. "See what grows back."

Lily was already moving, fingers dancing across her jade pendant as she cataloged injuries. She paused beside Clara, plucking a sprig of feverfew from her satchel. "Bleed on the artifacts again," she muttered, crushing leaves over the girl's raw wrists, "and I'll stitch your fingers together."

Tommy rolled onto his back, grinning through split lips. "C'mon darlin', ain't we all friends he—"

Deke's shadow swallowed him whole. "Next word," he said quietly, "is your last."

The valley chose that moment to breathe.

It started as a shiver through the sagebrush—leaves flipping silver-side up in unison. Then the light changed, sunlight fracturing into prismatic bands that made the warriors' obsidian blades hum. Aiyana's braids lifted as though underwater, strands floating in lazy spirals around the *wik'aani* tattooed across her collarbones.

"Shitfire," Tommy whispered.

Clara bucked against her bonds. "Ethan! The compa—"

Lily's palm clamped over her mouth, medicinal oils smothering the cry. "You've done enough."

But Ethan was already gone, drawn toward the shimmering air near the Three Sisters Terraces. His mother's compass burned against his hip, needle spinning wild circles. Through the warped light, figures moved— valley elders tending crops with antler tools. One stood apart.

Tall. Lean. Left shoulder canted like a doorframe with a sprung hinge.

Ethan's boots crushed sacred cornmeal offerings beneath him. The man turned.

Time fractured.

Same stubborn jawline. Same cowlick defying gray-streaked hair. Different eyes—not Ethan's prairie-sky blue, but the stormcloud gray from Grandma's daguerreotype.

"Hello, little cartographer." The voice cracked like old saddle leather.

Ethan's fist connected before he'd decided to swing. The man staggered into a basket of amaranth seeds, sending up crimson plumes.

"Easy, son."

"Don't." Ethan's knuckles throbbed. "You don't get to call me that."

The man rubbed his jaw, revealing a scar Ethan knew by heart—four white dashes above the thumb. From the summer Ethan, at six, had tried "helping" with the ax.

"Your mother's journals," the man said quietly. "Page eighty-four."

Blood pounded in Ethan's ears. He saw the entry clearer than yesterday's trail—sketch of bear grass flowers, margin note in Mom's cramped script: *Gone to find where maps end. Forgive me.*

The compass needle snapped due north.

"She didn't write that." Ethan's throat tightened. "You did."

Around them, the Valley's Breath intensified. Swirling pollen caught fire without burning, casting the terraces in foxfire green. Somewhere behind Ethan, Deke barked orders. Hooves pounded earth. None of it mattered.

The man reached into his elk-hide shirt, withdrawing a tobacco tin Ethan remembered kicking across cabin floorboards. Inside lay a lock of chestnut hair tied with cavalry cord. Mom's. Always Mom's.

"Stayed away to protect you," the man said. "From the Legion. From... this." He gestured at the luminous fields. "Should've known Anna's boy would find it anyway."

Ethan's knees hit fertile soil. "Eighteen years."

"Three wars here." Calloused fingers brushed his shoulder—same tentative gesture as when teaching him to track mule deer. "One for the land. One for our souls. One..." The pause stretched between them like barbed wire. "For family."

A gunshot ripped the air.

Both men wheeled toward camp. Tommy danced backward, Deke's stolen Colt smoking in his grip. Two warriors lay sprawled in the sacred White Clay deposits, dark stains spreading through mineral veins.

"Now!" Tommy screamed at Clara. "Move your ass!"

The girl lunged sideways, bound wrists slashing toward Aiyana's throat. Her weapon? Granddaddy's journal—pages splayed open to reveal glinting steel teeth sewn into the binding.

Lily's herb knife flashed. Paper guts rained down.

"Fascinating," she deadpanned, pinning Clara with a knee between the shoulder blades. "Did you read the chapter on tetanus?"

The valley's luminescence dimmed. Warriors closed ranks. Tommy swung the Colt toward Ethan.

Click.

Deke's Marlin .45 answered from ten paces. "Game's done, gambler."

Tommy squinted down the barrel. "Hell, O'Sullivan. Thought you couldn't shoot left-handed."

"Learned last Tuesday."

The crack of gunpowder merged with the thunderclap of returning magic. Tommy dropped. Clara wailed. And through the chaos, Ethan felt his father's hand steady on his back—warm, trembling, unbearably familiar.

"They'll need you," the man murmured.

Ethan stared at the smoking revolver in his own grip. When had he drawn it? "Need us both," he rasped.

Somewhere in the luminous haze, a warrior began the death chant.

***

The valley's luminescence surged like a struck match. Ethan's fingers went slack around the revolver as the ghostly fog writhed between him and the weathered face he'd last seen twelve winters past. Same hawk nose. Same scar through the left eyebrow. Different eyes—hollowed by years Ethan couldn't account for.

"You died." The words tasted like gun oil. "Ma buried an empty box."

Samuel Blake's calloused hand hovered near Ethan's elbow, not quite touching. "Your mother understood debts." Behind them, warriors murmured as the White Clay deposits began shimmering where blood had spilled. "This valley collects what's owed."

Aiyana materialized through the luminous haze, her braids crackling with static. "The Breath recognizes blood ties." She eyed Samuel like a misplaced puzzle piece. "Even tangled ones."

The ground hummed. Clara's wails cut off mid-shriek as tendrils of mist coiled around her thrashing legs. Tommy groaned through shattered teeth, the fog probing his wound with clinical curiosity.

"Christ almighty," Deke muttered, backing away from a glowing clay vein snaking toward his boots. "Place's gone woke."

Lily crouched by the pulsating earth, jade pendant swinging. "Fascinating. Hematophagic mineral absorption." She glanced at Samuel. "You been feeding it long?"

"Enough." Samuel's jaw tightened. "Son..."

Ethan stepped back. The revolver felt foreign now. "You left us scraping for Army contracts while you played shaman?"

Thunder rippled through clear sky. The mist solidified into towering figures—warriors on horseback, their outlines blurring across decades. A phantom stagecoach rattled past bearing the Blake family crest.

Samuel grimaced. "I tried shielding you from the Legion's mess."

"By making me clean it?" Ethan's laugh bit deeper than any bullet. The spectral images shifted—Sarah Blake scribbling journals by lantern light, young Ethan tracing maps with charcoal-stained fingers.

Aiyana gripped her obsidian blade as the visions intensified. "The land remembers what men forget."

Clara screamed. The mist had reached her waist now, leaching color from her dress. Tommy made wet choking sounds as his blood levitated toward the hungry clay.

"Enough!" Samuel roared. The valley stilled. Even the warrior's death chant faltered. "Take your pound of flesh tomorrow. Let the boy have tonight."

The Breath shuddered. For three heartbeats, every shadow held the shape of Civil War trenches. Then the mist dissipated, leaving only starlight and the coppery tang of grudges postponed.

Deke spat. "Well that's a new brand of horseshit."

Lily examined Tommy's paused bleeding. "Fascinating hemostatic properties."

Ethan stared at the man who'd carved his first compass. The man who'd missed his first shave. Who smelled of pine resin instead of Ma's lavender soap.

"Tomorrow," Ethan said flatly.

Samuel nodded. "Fair enough."

As warriors led the prisoners away, Aiyana pressed a palm to the settling clay. "Mind your balance, Blake blood." Her eyes reflected centuries older than her face. "Valleys drown loud footsteps."

Ethan reloaded his revolver. The cylinder clicked with finality. "We done here?"

Somewhere in the pines, a lone harmonica began playing *Darling Nelly Gray*. The exact way Pa used to.

"Not even close," Samuel muttered.

Overhead, the northern lights twisted into something that looked like a smirk.

CHAPTER 12

Sins of the Father

T HE VALLEY'S ETERNAL MIST curled around Ethan's boots like ghosts trying to drag him underground. Twenty feet ahead, a man emerged from the spectral haze wearing his dead father's face.

"Been waiting for you to find your way," James Blake said, voice frayed at the edges like sun-rotted rope. His beard had gone wolf-gray, eyes the same glacial blue as the thermal pools dotting the valley floor.

Ethan's fingers found the Colt at his hip, thumb brushing cold steel. Muscle memory. Reassurance. "You look like hell."

James barked a laugh that startled a pair of ravens from the pines. "Your mother always said that was my best color." He took a step forward, boot sinking deep in loam that released the sharp scent of crushed sage. "This place... it's not just land, Ethan. It's a goddamn beating heart."

A muscle twitched in Ethan's jaw. "We buried an empty coffin."

"Had to."

"Had to?" The words came out strangled. Ethan's left hand flexed, craving the weight of an ax handle, a shovel, anything to channel the tremor working up his arm. "Ma cried herself blind. Sarah stopped speaking for a year. You *had to?*"

James peeled back his sheepskin coat, revealing a puckered scar over his ribs. "First month I tried leaving? Got jumped by three men where Silver Creek forks. Bastards carried Langston iron." His calloused fingers brushed the ruined flesh. "Valley doesn't let go easy once it's got teeth in you."

Ethan spat into the moss. "So you chose dirt over blood."

"Chose keeping poison out of the world's veins!" James' shout sent ripples across a nearby pool, the strange blue water sloshing against lichen-crusted stones. "What's growing here... those plants cured the Spanish Flu outbreak in '19. Stopped the diphtheria that took the Blackfeet camp last winter. You think men like Victor Langston would let that lie fallow?"

The wind shifted, carrying the metallic tang of gun oil.

Ethan's spine straightened a half-second before the shot cracked through the valley. A bullet whined off granite six inches from James' head.

"Company," Ethan growled, already moving.

Chaosis erupted in plumes of birds taking flight. Thirty riders poured through the eastern pass, their Winchesters glinting like a steel thicket. At the vanguard rode Victor Langston, his tailored waistcoat straining across broad shoulders, silver-streaked hair slicked back beneath a Stetson that cost more than most farms.

"Gentlemen!" Langston's voice carried the polished malice of a courtroom executioner. "How fortuitous to find both Blakes in one grave."

Aiyana materialized from the mist, her obsidian braids threaded with gull feathers. "You bring rifles to a sanctuary," she said, calm as stone.

Langston's smile showed too many teeth. "I bring progress to a garden, madam. Imagine what proper cultivation could—"

Ethan's Colt cleared leather with a snake's hiss. "You imagine lead through your spleen?"

The valley held its breath. Somewhere in the pines, a pinecone cracked open in the sudden silence.

Langston adjusted his cufflinks. "Charming. But I've brought dinner guests." He gestured westward where tendrils of black smoke began coiling above the treeline. The acidic stench of burning yarrow hit Ethan's nostrils—medicinal fields ablaze.

James lunged for the nearest rider, a kid barely old enough to shave. The crack of breaking cartilage merged with the first screams as valley dwellers streamed from their lodges, clutching children and herb bundles.

Ethan sighted down his barrel at Langston's smirking mouth. "You're holding a lit match to dynamite, you bastard."

"Then by all means," Langston purred, spreading his arms wide, "let's watch the world burn together."

***

The valley's screams tasted like copper against Lily's tongue. She pressed her thumb into the jade pendant's weathered grooves as smoke stung her eyes—not from Langston's fires, but from the valley itself weeping. The silk cord bit her neck as she spun toward a stand of quaking aspens. Their leaves chattered warnings in ultraviolet.

"Xiǎo xīn!" The Mandarin slipped out as her palm met peeling bark. Her pendant burned cold against collarbones. Roots whispered through her bootsoles—a fungal network screaming in silent agony where Langston's men trampled sacred ground. Visions flashed behind her molars: mycorrhizal threads connecting ghost orchids to ponderosa pines, medicinal moss codes older than Babylon.

A gunshot cracked. The bullet hit dirt six inches left of her boot. Lily didn't flinch. Milkweed vines erupted from the earth, thorns shredding the shooter's pantlegs as she sprinted toward the healing huts.

"Blake!" She caught Ethan mid-stride, his Smith & Wesson trained on three riders torching a yarrow field. "This isn't just plants. It's a keystone web." Her fingers dug into his forearm. "Kill this ecosystem, half the continent's medicinal..."

Ethan shook her off, eyes locked on Langston's gleeful arsonists. "Tell that to the bastards roasting our pharmacy."

The pendant throbbed. Lily grabbed his chin, forcing eye contact. "That goldenrod you're standing on? Only pollinator for seventy miles. These firs?" She kicked a sapling. "Rainmakers. Burn this valley, next drought starves ten territories."

His jaw muscle jumped. Somewhere behind them, a scream cut off wetly.

James Blake materialized through smoke, his Remington smoking. "Son. The eastern gulch—"

"Don't." Ethan's knuckles whitened on his revolver. "You don't get to command shit."

Aiyana's war cry split the air as she rode bareback through flames, her bone club caving in a mercenary's skull. Deke emerged from the chaos dragging two kids by their collars. His shotgun spoke twice—a horseman crumpled.

"Playtime's over." Deke spat blood near James' boots. "Need to bleed Langston's numbers." He jerked his chin westward. "Cave system past Dead Man's Gully. Lure 'em in, collapse the throat."

Ethan's laugh held broken glass. "Since when do you volunteer for suicide runs?"

"Since always." Deke's grin didn't touch his eyes. He palmed a stick of railroad dynamite from his coat—old Union Pacific stamp still visible. "Just prefer company when I dance with devils."

Lily's pendant seared ice-fire. She gripped Deke's wrist. "The caves...bat colony there synthesizes anticoagulants in their guano. Lose that—"

"Plague outbreaks from here to Santa Fe," Deke finished. His calloused thumb brushed her pulse point. "Know the cost, Miss Chen."

James stepped between them. "I'll flank—"

Ethan's fist connected with his father's cheekbone. "You'll stay the hell away from my people." Blood dripped between them like a challenge.

Deke checked his Colt's cylinder. "Family reunions later. Corpses mounting now." He tossed Ethan a stick of dynamite. "Still throw like Princeton boy?"

The fuse hissed to life in Ethan's grip. "Better than you track, O'Sullivan."

As the dynamite arc lit up screaming horses, Lily's pendant showed her three possible futures in the darting fireflies—all required a blood price. She began unraveling her silk cord.

"Medic!" someone shouted.

"Coming!" Lily lied, weaving poison oak through gunpowder trails. The valley's roots coiled in her marrow, teaching vengeance.

***

The valley hummed like a plucked bowstring. Ethan spat blood in the dirt where he'd punched his father, then turned to the real work. "Chen— poison oak along the eastern ridge. O'Sullivan needs clear paths marked."

Lily didn't look up from braiding wolfsbane into tripwire. "Already seeding stinging nettle gullies. Your mother's journals mention cave sulfur deposits?"

"North shelf." Ethan tossed her a leather satchel full of rusted mining tags. "Mark the unstable tunnels."

Across the clearing, Deke methodically ruined a good knife. The blade sawed through fuse cord while his left hand palmed railroad detonators like communion wafers. Each click of the primer caps carried memories best left buried—stagecoach strongboxes popping open, Pinkerton men screaming through gunpowder fog. His thumb traced the Celtic cross notched into the Colt's grip. Redemption tasted like salt and blasting powder tonight.

"Need three volunteers!" Ethan barked.

A Blackfoot elder materialized with two teens carrying elk-horn bows. "We hunt shadows."

Deke stood abruptly, dynamite bundles crisscrossing his chest like bandoliers. "You follow *my trail markers*. Step off the cairns, you'll be picking your teeth out of pines."

The elder's smile showed three missing molars. "We know ghost-walker sign."

Ethan gripped Deke's shoulder—too hard for comfort, too brief for sentiment. "Flush them toward the sinkholes."

"Wasn't planning tea service." Deke checked the wind direction with a wet finger. The pendant around Lily's neck pulsed once, casting jade light across his scarred knuckles. He wondered if saints felt this cold certainty before the lion's den.

Lily intercepted him at the tree line, hands full of thorned vines. "Mountain laurel. Chew one leaf every two hours counteracts swamp gas hallucinations."

"Trying to keep me lucid, Miss Chen?"

"Trying to keep you from blowing up the wrong canyon." Her fingernails left half-moon indents in his wrist. "The fire moss colonies can't handle another burn year."

Deke tucked the leaves into his bandana. "Tell Princeton boy to watch his six. Langston prefers backshots." He melted into the aspens without disturbing the moth perched on a branch.

Back at camp, Ethan was mapping kill zones with charcoal on cured hide. Lily crouched beside him, her hair snagging on his stubble when she pointed. "This meadow's false hellebore can induce paralysis if we funnel them through the pollen clouds."

"Set up wind traps with the spare canvas." Ethan's pencil snapped mid-sentence. "And your father's black powder formulas—"

"—are already rigged to the irrigation sluices." Lily pressed a hand over his racing pulse. "Breathe, Blake. The land fights with us."

He stilled under her touch. "My mother's journals... Did she ever..."

"Page forty-two." Lily placed a dog-eared journal in his hands. "'When the valley's bones ache, listen through stone.' Your margin notes disagree."

Ethan's choked laugh sounded suspiciously like hope. "I wrote that?"

"Princeton arrogance." Her boot nudged his shin. "Turns out granite *does* sing in C-sharp during earth tremors."

They strung barbed wire through stands of poison sumac as dawn bled across the cliffs. Somewhere north, three consecutive explosions shook loose a waterfall of scree. Every bird in the valley took wing at once—a feathered hurricane blotting out the stars.

Lily counted heartbeats until the echo died. "O'Sullivan's on schedule."

Ethan tested the garrote wire's tension. "He better be late to his own funeral."

Above them, the night bloomed gunpowder orange.

***

The copper tang of black powder clung to Ethan's teeth as he adjusted the tripwire strung between two ancient pines. Somewhere below the ridge line, a red-tailed hawk screamed its territory claim three times - Aiyana's sentry signal. All clear. For now.

James emerged from the spruce shadows holding two tin cups. Steam curled around the old man's calloused fingers. "Your mother always said coffee tasted better when death might interrupt it."

Ethan kept his eyes on the knotted wire. "She tell you that before or after you faked your corpse?"

The tin cup appeared in his peripheral vision. "Two sugars. Like when you were twelve."

The familiar sweet-bitter bite flooded Ethan's mouth with memories he'd rather choke on. "You missed the part where I started taking it black."

James huffed something that almost passed for laughter. "Noted." He crouched beside Ethan, examining the garrote-wire patterns with a tracker's eye. "Sarah's work?"

"Modified." Ethan jerked his chin toward the poison sumac thicket downslope. "Lily's additions."

"Smart." James traced a finger along the tripwire's anchor point. His nail showed the same crescent-shaped scar Ethan remembered from childhood - split kindling with a dull hatchet. "These high lines'll funnel them into the kill zone."

Ethan's gut tightened. "That the voice of experience talking?"

"Voice of a man who's spent ten years protecting this dirt." James stood abruptly, coffee sloshing over the rim. "You think I wanted—"

A conch shell blast echoed up the canyon. Two short, one long. Langston's vanguard had breached the eastern gullies.

James froze mid-sentence, face hardening into the leathery mask Ethan remembered from hunting trips gone wrong. "They're early."

"Or Deke's late." Ethan spat coffee grounds onto the pine needles. His hand found the Winchester '73 leaning against the tree - walnut stock worn smooth from a thousand similar grips.

Down in the valley bowl, Aiyana's war cry rose above the sudden clamor of cocking rifles and clicking breechblocks. Defenders melted into firing positions among the terraced fields, their movements precise as a barn-raising crew. Old Chen tested the wind with a damp thumb before lighting the warning beacons - blue-tinged flames licking at pine pitch bundles.

Lily appeared at Ethan's elbow smelling of crushed mint and gunsmoke. "Main force's still two ridges back. That's just Langston's advance scouts." Her jade pendant caught the firelight as she pointed northwest. "Deke's herding them toward the scree slopes."

Another conch blast - three staccato bleats. Closer this time.

James checked his Spencer carbine's rotary magazine. "Scouts'll have field glasses. They see those terraces..."

"Already handled." Lily nodded to where Aiyana's warriors were draping camouflage netting over the Three Sisters crops. "Migrant workers taught us how to hide an entire railroad camp from Pinkertons."

Ethan caught the faint tremor in her fingers as she adjusted the barbed wire barricades. He pressed the dog-eared journal into her hands. "Page forty-two's yours if—"

"Don't." Her palm slapped against his chest, right over the ragged bullet scar beneath his shirt. "We're both walking out of this."

The night exploded in gunfire.

Twenty yards downhill, a flaming arrow lodged in a Ponderosa's sap blisters. Orange light bloomed across the slope, revealing dark shapes advancing in skirmish formation. Someone screamed in Blackfoot. A Winnebago war club arced through the firelight, met a sickening crunch.

Ethan sighted down the Winchester's barrel. "Here we—"

The entire mountainside shuddered. Boulders the size of stagecoaches peeled away from the cliffs above Langston's position. Deke's diversion - the Irishman had triggered the avalanche charges early.

Through the rolling dust cloud, Ethan glimpsed shadowy figures scattering like quail. A harmonica's shrill note pierced the chaos - Deke's all-clear signal.

"Move!" Ethan grabbed Lily's arm as the first rocks crashed through the treeline. They dove behind a granite outcrop as the world dissolved into flying splinters and pulverized stone.

When the dust settled, an unnatural quiet blanketed the slope. Ethan spat grit, tasting blood. The Winchester's barrel glowed faint orange from rapid fire.

Lily peered over the rock's jagged edge. "Holy mother of—"

Where Langston's scouts had stood, a fresh scree field stretched fifty yards wide. Moonlight glinted off buried rifle barrels and the occasional boot heel protruding from the rubble.

Aiyana's voice cut through the ringing silence. "Second wave incoming! West ridge!"

Ethan followed her pointing knife. Beyond the settling dust, a dark smear rippled across the moonlit prairie - hundreds of mounted figures advancing at a trot. The ground itself seemed to undulate beneath their boots.

Lily's nails dug into his forearm. "That's no scouting party."

"Main assault." Ethan reloaded with shells from his dead father's ammunition belt. "Right on schedule."

Somewhere in the advancing horde, a Gatling gun coughed its mechanical laugh. Cottonwood saplings disintegrated six feet to their left.

James appeared beside them, bleeding from a scalp wound. "Fall back to the terrace trenches!"

"Like hell." Ethan chambered a round. "This is the choke point."

"The hell it is." James hauled him upright with surprising strength. "You die here, the whole flank collapses!"

Another Gatling burst chewed through the pine they'd been using for cover. Splinters rained down as they scrambled upslope.

Lily's boot slipped on loose shale. "Ethan!"

He caught her wrist an inch from a sixty-foot drop. For three heartbeats they dangled over emptiness, her jade pendant swinging wildly. Then strong hands hauled them both to safety - Aiyana and two Blackfoot warriors wordlessly anchoring the rescue chain.

The terrace trenches stank of sweat and coal oil. Defenders crouched behind stacked grain sacks, passing ammunition like communion wine. Old Chen distributed arrows fletched with owl feathers while humming a Canton sea shanty.

Ethan pressed against the packed earth berm, counting shadows in the killing field below. Two hundred yards. One-fifty. The metallic click of seventy rifles cocking in unison rolled through the valley.

Aiyana nocked a broadhead. "Wait for the false hellebore bloom."

The first mortar shell hit the upper pastures.

Dirt rained down as the concussion wave rattled teeth. Ethan's "Hold position!" got drowned by screaming livestock and the Gatling gun's renewed appetite.

Lithgow rifles barked from the trench line. Two riders dropped. Three. A team of draft horses veered into a concealed punji stake pit, their death screams merging with the gunfire.

"Wind's shifting!" Lily pressed her pendant to a flowering stalk of false hellebore. The plant's petals glowed faint green before detonating in a pollen cloud that glimmered like evil stardust.

Riders began choking mid-stride. Langston's advance faltered as men clawed at swelling throats. Aiyana's archers picked off the stumbling figures with methodical precision.

Ethan allowed himself three seconds of hope. Then the mountain behind them erupted.

White-phosphorus mortar rounds lit up the Sentinel Range like demonic fireworks. Through the cascading flames, Ethan glimpsed Langston's personal banner - a silver wolf's head snapping in the heat waves.

The last thing he heard before the world went white was Lily's curse and the stomach-churning whine of artillery shells in flight.

CHAPTER 13

Lines in the Sand

ETHAN'S BOOTS CARVED ANGRY grooves into the dirt at the valley's edge. The Blake compass bit into his palm where he gripped it too tight—a brass-and-oak bruise against his calluses. *Twenty paces east, pivot, nineteen back west.* Numbers clicked behind his teeth like rifle shells. Every rotation brought the jagged peaks of the Sentinel Range into view, stone teeth ready to chew through whatever came crawling out of Silver Creek.

A granite pebble skittered underfoot. He caught himself mid-stumble, the sudden lurch yanking his thoughts clear. "Hell." The word hung between cliff walls. His mother's journals had described the Ghost Walker's Dance—those ground-hugging mists coiling like jealous lovers around the valley—but seeing the fog thicken ten feet below where he paced? That turned book ink into bile rising in his throat.

"Still arguing with the horizon?"

Aiyana's voice cut through without sharpness. She stood five paces off, arms folded in sleeves stitched with stormcloud patterns. The braids framing her face held fresh owl feathers today. Warning or blessing? Ethan couldn't tell.

He snapped the compass shut. "Trying to calculate sightlines. Langston's men'll come armed with more than pickaxes this time."

"Mmh." She crouched, fingers brushing sagebrush. "Your mother's maps showed old mudslides north of Three Sisters terraces. Reroute the western creekbed there, and the earth remembers how to swallow greed."

Ethan's thumb found the compass's needle groove. Water warfare—crude but clever. "We'd need to collapse the upper banks."

"Already sent trackers to weaken the ledges." Aiyana rose, dusk-colored wool skirts whispering. "Unless you'd rather wait for their dynamite?"

A chuckle escaped him—dry as August grass. "When you're right, you're right."

"Often am." Her eyes crinkled. "But you knew that when you asked for N'mm̂íí water tactics instead of cavalry charges."

The truth of it warmed his chest. Sarah Blake's journals had called the Blackfoot earth-shapers 'terrain tacticians.' Turned out they wrote the damn book.

***

Lily Chen's knee screamed. She ignored it, bootheel grinding into scree as she scaled the third terrace. The jade pendant bounced hot between her collarbones—not quite burning, but insistent. Like Ma tapping her shoulder during exams back in San Francisco.

"Xiǎo xīn!" The warning slipped out as her boot dislodged a rock. Below, two hidden society scouts glanced up. She flashed three fingers—Chen family code for *keep working*. They returned to planting devil's club thickets along the irrigation ditch. Good. Thorns bought time.

Her field journal flapped against her hip. Page fourteen bore yesterday's sketch of Aiyana's shockroot—tubers that exploded toxic pollen when disturbed. Now she scribbled over the illustration: *Mix with pine resin? Adhesive irritant traps.* The pendant's heat pulsed agreement.

A scout offered a canteen. Lily shook her head, thumb already testing milkweed sap viscosity on her wrist. "Gather blisterpod," she ordered.

"Three baskets. And find Deke. Tell him I need his whetstone."

The man blinked. "For herbs?"

"No," she deadpanned, crushing a dried stinger vine into powder. "For comedy. Move."

***

Deke materialized between two aspens like the forest spat him out. Mud streaked his duster. So did blood—not his, judging by the easy prowl of his gait.

"Y'all cozy?" He lobbed a rusted tin toward Ethan's feet.

Aiyana caught it mid-air. Rot spread iron-scented as she pried the lid open. Sheriff's star inside. Tarnished. Cracked across the bear emblem.

Ethan went very still.

"Found that nailed to Whiterock's telegraph post." Deke's Irish bled through thicker than usual. "With a message. *'Seven dawns. Bring the cartographer.'*"

Wind riffled the pages of Lily's journal as she arrived, sleeves crusted in alkaloid powders. "Sam Hart's badge."

"Was his." Deke spat. "Till he sold your coordinates for Langston's gold."

Lily's fingers brushed the jade pendant. "You're certain?"

"Tracked him to Silver Creek's new cathouse. He's wearing deputy iron now." Deke's smile showed teeth. "Knew the bastard's whiskey stench from forty paces."

Ethan stared at the broken star. Sam's laugh echoed in memory—warm as a campfire, two winters back when they'd driven off claim-jumpers together. The man had thrown an arm around his shoulders, crowing *'Justice tastes better shared!'*

Now the compass weighed heavy. North needle quivered. Not toward magnetic pole, but the valley's heart. Always here.

"Burn the cathouse?" Deke's hand rested on his Sharps rifle.

"No." Ethan snapped the compass open. True north glimmered beneath etched glass. "We let Sam deliver his lies."

Aiyana nodded. "And when Langston comes?"

Around them, the Ghost Walker's Dance swirled higher. Somewhere downslope, a shockroot pod burst. Scouts shouted in triumph.

Lily rubbed sap-stained fingers together. "We remind them what happens to blight in healthy soil."

***

Ethan's thumb traced the compass lid where Sam Hart had once carved **_JUSTICE_** with a bowie knife. The letters felt colder now. "Seven dawns," he muttered, staring at the fractured badge in his palm. The silver caught afternoon light wrong—tainted, like creek water shimmering over rot.

Deke leaned against a shockroot tree, whittling a stick to splinters. "Gonna piss on his grave or water the roses with him?"

"Neither." Ethan snapped the compass shut. Memory flickered—Sam's hand gripping his shoulder two winters back after they'd cornered rustlers in a box canyon. _'You're decent company for a map-worshiper,'_ the sheriff had grinned, breath fogging in the cold. Now that same breath reeked of Langston's coin.

Lily crouched nearby, mortar grinding bittercap roots to paste. "Betrayal's a seed," she said without looking up. "Let it root, it strangles everything." Her jade pendant glinted toxic green as she poured the paste into clay ampoules.

"Wisdom from the Chen family almanac?" Deke drawled.

"Common sense from anyone who's cleared blightweed." She tossed him an ampoule. "Flash-bangs. Try not to inhale."

Aiyana emerged from the terraces, James Blake trailing her like a shadow made flesh. The old man's hands were stained indigo from woad dye, maps of veins standing raised beneath parchment skin. "The Three

Sisters remember," he announced, voice rasping like wheat stalks in wind. "Defenses older than your railroads."

Ethan straightened. "Show us."

***

James led them to the western ledge where the Living Terraces cascaded downslope. He pressed gnarled fingers against a seam in the stone. With a groan older than prayer, a section of cliff face swung inward—revealing channels cut precise as surgeon's incisions.

"Aqueducts," Lily breathed, running her hand along moss-slick grooves. "But the gradient..."

"Terraced cisterns." James tapped a finger against his temple. "Flood the upper reservoirs, and the valley becomes a waterfall. Washes away pests." His milky eyes found Ethan's. "If you're willing to drown your enemies."

Deke snorted. "Langston's men can't swim worth shit. I'm in."

Aiyana studied the mechanism. "The People used these against the Blackfoot in the Bad Winter."

"And lost," James countered.

"We're still here." She gripped a lever grown smooth from generations of hands. "Are you afraid of history, Ethan Blake?"

He watched a leaf spiral into the dark channel. Saw Sam's face in the eddies. "Can we control the flow?"

James smiled, teeth yellow as old ivory. "Control's an illusion. But direction?" He spat into the aqueduct. The phlegm raced downhill, vanishing into shadow. "That we can manage."

***

Work began at moonrise. The hidden society emerged from cliff dwellings and root cellars—silent men and women carrying pickaxes worn smooth from carving stone. Ethan marveled at their precision. No orders barked, just the soft clink of tools and occasional burst of laughter when someone misjudged a pulley line.

Lily rigged tripwires with tanglethorn vines. "Step here," she explained to a wide-eyed boy no older than twelve, "and the vines constrict. Slows them enough for—"

"For shooting," the boy finished, hefting a slingshot. "Ma says I'm death on rabbits."

"Aim for the eyes," Deke advised, passing by with an armload of quarrels. "Rabbits scream prettier."

Ethan found Aiyana atop the highest terrace, directing teams in a language that clicked and trilled like falling pebbles. She paused when he approached. "Your Sheriff Hart—did he ever speak of lightning?"

"Once." Ethan recalled a campfire tale about Sam chasing tornadoes as a boy. "Said storms called to him."

Aiyana nodded toward the eastern ridges. "Good. Let him remember that fear."

Following her gaze, Ethan saw the first tendrils of Ghost Walker's Dance coiling through the pines. The unnatural fog moved against the wind, glowing faintly blue where moonlight pierced its folds. It pooled in ravines, climbed trunks like liquid, until the entire valley seemed encased in spectral glass.

James materialized beside them, smelling of damp clay and camphor. "Land knows," he whispered. "Feels the sickness coming."

Below, Deke's voice carried upslope as he taught settlers to notch arrows. "Draw till your momma's ghost pinches your ear! Steady...steady..."

Lily appeared, sleeves rolled to reveal forearms mapped in chemical burns. She handed Ethan a smoke bomb sealed with beeswax. "Sam taught you to track storms. Use that."

"Against him?"

"Against what he's become." She pressed the bomb into his palm. Her fingers left soot smudges shaped like constellations. "Men like Langston?

131

They're kudzu. Choke everything unless burned clean."

The mist thickened. Somewhere in its depths, a wolf howled—or maybe just the wind through canyon teeth. Ethan gripped the compass until the etched metal bit his skin. North still pointed valley-ward. Always would.

"Hart comes at dawn," he said.

Aiyana placed a hand on the aqueduct lever. "Let him bring his storm."

They waited as the Ghost Walker's Dance swallowed the stars.

***

The valley hummed like a plucked bowstring. Ethan traced the compass needle across his palm, its etched directions merging with calluses earned mapping deadlier terrain than this. Twenty yards downhill, three Blackfoot elders argued over how to angle mirrored shields stolen from Langston's supply train.

"Tell 'em south by southeast," Deke muttered, spitting tobacco near Ethan's boot. "Canyon bounce'll fry Hart's scouts crispier than preacher bacon."

Ethan studied the play of blue-tinged mist across copper reflectors. "Aiyana says wait until the Ghost Dance reaches Sentinel Rock."

"Your ghost fog got a timetable?"

"It did when you needed cover to raid Langston's armory."

Deke's grin flashed wolfish. He tossed Ethan a revolver wrapped in oilskin. "Special delivery. Modified chambers for Lily's poison darts."

The weapon stank of crushed monkshood petals. Ethan thumbed the unfamiliar trigger guard. "She distill the toxin herself?"

"While lecturing some settler brat on proper fern identification." Deke jerked his chin toward the terraces. "Go see your walking apothecary. These cranky bastards won't listen unless you smirk less."

***

Lily knelt between squash vines, charcoal stick flying across bark paper. Her journal pages fluttered with diagrams—arrowhead molds, pressure plate schematics, chemical formulas that made Ethan's eyes water.

"Deke says you're arming toddlers now," he said.

She didn't look up. "Mrs. Oleson's daughters can calculate trajectory better than your riflemen." Her jade pendant swung, casting leaf-shaped shadows over notes about acidic lichen. "Help me shift this log. The beetles underneath secrete numbing agents."

They heaved the rotting pine. A seething mass of iridescent carapaces scattered. Lily snatched two beetles mid-flight, popping them into a bamboo tube.

"Extract enough toxin," she said, "and we'll drop invaders where they stand."

"Assuming they don't shoot first."

Her smile cut sharper than skinning knives. "Let them." She pressed the tube into his hand. Cold seeped through the bamboo. "Pain's a great teacher."

Aiyana's conch horn moaned across the valley. Three short blasts— scouts sighted. Lily was already moving, shouting orders to a chain of teenagers manning the aqueduct pulleys. Her braid unraveled as she ran, dark hair streaming like battle standard.

***

Deke found the trapper trying to piss behind a boulder. "Christ almighty, O'Hara. You water plants or kill 'em?"

The man fumbled his trousers. "Ain't no outhouses in war!"

"There's war and there's manners." Deke kicked the man's boot. "Upslope. Third cedar's got a nice privacy screen."

"Why the third?"

"First two are rigged with bear traps."

As O'Hara scrambled away, Deke crouched to examine trampled yarrow. Fresh boot prints overlapped deer tracks. Too wide for settlers. He whistled—three ascending notes. Two children materialized from a thicket, blowguns ready.

"South gully," Deke said. "Tell the mirror crew we got company sniffing around."

The girl nodded, plucked a thorn from her hair. "Bait?"

"Standard protocol."

Her brother grinned, hefting a woven cage full of enraged badgers. Deke tossed them a peppermint tin. "For the road. Sugar helps the aim."

***

Iron clanged on slate. Every head swiveled toward the sound. Ethan stood atop Sentinel Rock, hammering Langston's stolen pickaxe against stone. The valley held its breath.

"Positions!" he roared.

The terraces erupted in motion. Lily's toxin crews ducked behind fortified berms. Blackfoot archers melted into stands of quaking aspen. Deke's trackers unleashed six screaming badgers down the main trail, each daubed in skunk oil and chili paste.

Ethan leaped down, landing beside Aiyana at the aqueduct controls. Her hands hovered over levers carved with wolf sigils.

"Now?" she asked.

He watched tendrils of Ghost Walker's Dance curl around the highest pines. Mist thickened into opaque walls. Somewhere beyond the white veil, steel rattled against rock.

"Wait for the first shot," Ethan said.

Lily appeared at his left, face smeared with soot and something that glittered like crushed stars. She pressed a smoke bomb into Aiyana's hand. "For the cannons."

Deke took position on Ethan's right, reloading his modified revolver. "Bet Hart's wearing his good boots."

"You want them?"

"Nah. Just planning where to shoot."

A rifle cracked. Splinters exploded from a cedar trunk ten feet overhead.

Ethan smiled. "Right on time."

Aiyana threw the lever.

***

The aqueducts roared like awakened dragons. Ethan tasted copper-flavored mist as Ghost Walker's Dance thickened into a living wall between his people and Langston's cannons. Lily's smoke bombs detonated upstream, turning the Silver Creek tributary into a boiling mercury river that glowed unnaturally bright.

"Deke!" Ethan snapped.

"Already on it." The tracker lobbed a pinecone cluster into the chaos. Gunpowder resin flashed crimson when it hit the poisoned water. "Present for the assholes."

Aiyana gripped Ethan's forearm, her fingers digging into his buckskin sleeve. "The eastern ridge..."

Ethan followed her gaze. Mist curled away to reveal a dozen silhouettes cresting the high ground. He didn't blink. "Blake! You still got those fire wasps?"

His cousin's laugh carried through the din. James unleashed three clay spheres from his sling. They shattered against granite outcrops, releasing swarms that crackled like grease on a skillet. Men's screams turned soprano.

Lily materialized at Ethan's flank, jade pendant swinging wildly as she jammed fresh cartridges into her modified flare gun. "Hart's trying to flank the lower terrace."

"Let him." Ethan spat blood - he'd bitten his tongue during the last cannon volley. "Remember the sinkholes?"

Her grin flashed white through grime. She whistled sharply. Six Blackfoot teens yanked camouflaged levers. The ground swallowed twenty mercenaries mid-charge.

Deke ambushed Hart first.

The sheriff's custom spurs gave him away, jingling like a drunk's pocket change as he crept through serviceberry bushes. Deke's boot caught Hart's wrist as the lawman reached for his sidearm.

"Looking for this?" Deke twirled Hart's prized Colt. "Heard you're partial to left knees."

The gunshot echoed oddly through the mist. Hart folded like bad origami.

Ethan didn't watch the body drop. He was too busy reading the valley's breath - the way mist coiled tight around defenders while blinding attackers, how sudden downdrafts smothered Langston's fires. When the mine boss himself emerged roaring from the treeline, Ethan simply raised two fingers.

The land answered.

A curtain of Ghost Walker's Dance solidified between Ethan's forces and the advancing thugs. Through the shimmering veil, Langston's face purpled with impotent rage. His shouted threats came through distorted, like a man drowning in honey.

Lily pressed her shoulder against Ethan's. "It's holding."

"For now." He kept his eyes on the pulsating mist-wall. Somewhere beyond, the real battle loomed. But here, in this unnatural twilight, defenders caught their breath. A Blackfoot grandmother passed around elderberry wine. James demonstrated pressure points to wide-eyed Chinese miners. Deke confiscated another pair of fancy spurs.

Aiyana joined them, bearing a stone cup that steamed despite the cool air. "The valley drinks with its protectors."

Ethan drained the bitter brew in one swallow. Felt roots grow where his boots met soil. When the mist finally thinned, they'd all be standing on ground that remembered.

For now, they waited.

And the land waited with them.

CHAPTER 14

The Siege

T HE VALLEY WOKE TO rifle fire instead of birdsong. Ethan Blake's boot crushed an empty cartridge underheel as he scanned the eastern ridge—a dark seam of men and horses rippling along the horizon. No time for pretty speeches. He grabbed young Tommy by his suspenders, shoving him toward the boulder cluster. "Suppressing fire on the washout gully. Three-round intervals." The kid opened his mouth to argue. Ethan cocked his Spencer carbine one-handed. "Move or mulch."

In the scrub below, Langston's mercenaries fanned out like ticks on a stag. Ethan's posse melted into the landscape—miners who knew every pebble, Blackfoot trackers who'd painted war stripes with mica dust. They waited until the first Easterner boots hit the loose shale slope.

Ambush erupted in staggered bursts. A Chicago gunslinger took a Mohawk arrow through his cravat. Two Pinkertons tumbled into a pit lined with flint shards. Ethan put a .56 caliber round through a Gatling gun's water jacket, steam hissing like a gut-shot panther. "Relocate!" he barked, already scrambling uphill. Behind them, the rocky defile became a lead storm.

Lily Chen crouched behind a lightning-split pine, fingers combing soil. Bloodroot. Poison ivy. Stand of chokecherry saplings. She spat on her palm and ground yarrow leaves into paste, smearing it across a linen strip. "Here." She slapped the poultice on a wrangler's buckshot-grazed arm. "Don't scratch when it itches." Her jade pendant swung like a metronome as she crawled toward the game trail.

The attackers' left flank was pushing through serviceberry brush. Lily palmed dried buffalo bladder from her satchel, filling it with crushed death camas bulbs. Tossed the stinking pouch into the thicket. Horses screamed. Men vomited. She was already twenty yards east, braiding wild rose canes through juniper branches—nature's barbed wire growing inch-long thorns before the next volley hit.

Deke O'Sullivan smelled his brother before he saw him. Cheap bay rum and cheaper tobacco. There, in the smoky haze—Jasper's gold-capped grin flashing as he pistol-whipped a fallen defender. Same swagger from their Missouri days. Same snake tattoo curling up his neck. Deke's Henry rifle wavered.

Memories flickered—Jasper taking the fall for that Butterfield job. Jasper sharing last whiskey in a Carson City jail. The Springfield's stock felt suddenly heavy as a coffin lid. Then he saw the dynamite bundle on Jasper's belt.

"Christ alive." Deke spat, levering a fresh round. The shot clipped Jasper's ear instead of his skull. Deliberate miss. Warning cry stuck in his throat like a fishbone.

Jasper turned. Laughed. Drew his Navy Colt left-handed like always. "Baby brother! You owe me seven dollars from—"

Deke's second shot sparked off Jasper's belt buckle. The dynamite didn't blow—thank Mary and all saints—but it scattered into the creekbed. Jasper dove behind a supply wagon, shouting obscenities that could curdle milk. Deke racked the Henry's lever hard enough to bruise his palm. "Stay down, you bastard!"

No answer but pistol fire through oak barrels. Deke melted backward into the chokeberry bushes, heart hammering triple-time. Somewhere north, Ethan was yelling coordinates. West, Lily's botanical barriers groaned under cavalry hooves. Deke wiped sweat from his eyes. The snake tattoo haunted his sights.

***

Deke's boot heel ground into creek gravel as Jasper's laughter carried over gunfire. "Still can't shoot straight, little brother?"

The O'Sullivan boys faced each other across twenty yards of churned earth, Jasper's Navy Colt dangling carelessly from his fingers. Deke noted the fresh scar where his first bullet had grazed Jasper's ear—the same ear he'd once stitched up after a Dodge City brothel fight.

"Should've aimed lower." Jasper tapped his belt where Deke's second shot had struck. "Might've saved Ma some shame."

Deke's knuckles whitened on the Henry rifle. "She died thinkin' you were dead. Let's keep it that way."

A cavalry charge thundered past Jasper's position, spooking the draft horses hitched to Langston's ammunition wagon. In the chaos, Deke saw his opening—three quick steps brought him behind a shattered water trough as Jasper's bullets chewed splinters from the wood.

"Remember the Jameson job?" Jasper called, reloading with theatrical slowness. "You froze then too."

"Different now." Deke lobbed a whiskey flask from his hip pocket—the one Jasper had gifted him on his sixteenth birthday. It arced over the trough, sunlight glinting on engraved initials.

Jasper caught it reflexively. Frowned at the 'D.O'S' etching. That heartbeat of distraction cost him—Deke's rifle butt smashed into his solar plexus, sending them both crashing into the shallows. Cold creekwater soaked Jasper's fancy waistcoat as they grappled, the stink of gunsmoke and river algae thick between them.

"You're protecting nothing but fools and dirt," Jasper spat, knee aiming for Deke's groin. "Langston's offering—"

Deke's forehead cracked against Jasper's nose. "Not for sale."

Three hundred yards northeast, Clara Benson pressed herself against the splintered remains of Crossroads Trading Post's west wall. Her red bandana itched with sweat as she eavesdropped on two of Langston's lieutenants arguing beside a Gatling gun emplacement.

"—flank them through the old landslide chute at dusk," growled the taller man, his Stetson shadowing a face pockmarked by smallpox. "Burn what's left."

Clara's calloused fingers dug into sunbaked adobe. That chute led straight to the hidden grain silos where half the valley's children sheltered. Her pulse roared louder than the nearby cannon fire.

"Hey! Ranch girl!"

She turned to see young Tommy Peabody gaping at her from a sniper's perch, his Sharps rifle forgotten. The boy had witnessed her midnight meetings with Langston's scouts. Seen the silver coins change hands.

Clara's hand flew to her holster. Stopped. Instead, she ripped the red bandana from her neck and tossed it up to him. "Tell Ethan Blake— landslide chute at dusk. You hear?"

Tommy's nod was barely perceptible. As Clara spun toward the defenders' lines, a Minie ball tore through her left calf. She hit the dirt cursing, crawling behind a burnt-out seed drill as bullets kicked dust around her.

"Goddamn stupid heroic bullshit," she muttered through gritted teeth, using her belt as a tourniquet. The Blake homestead's smokehouse loomed sixty yards ahead—sixty yards of open killing field.

She ran limping, howling a Comanche war cry she'd learned from old Chief Two Moons. Lead whined past her ears like angry hornets.

***

Ethan Blake didn't look up from his mother's hand-drawn maps when Clara collapsed bleeding at his feet. "Tommy signaled five minutes ago." His boot traced a contour line on the parchment. "They'll bottleneck here."

Lily Chen appeared like a vengeant spirit, mortar and pestle already grinding yarrow leaves into paste. "We need twenty minutes."

"Get seven." Ethan snapped his father's brass-cased compass shut. "Hank! Take six men to the shale slope. Use the rock drills from the Silver Creek mine."

A grizzled prospector spit tobacco. "Them augers ain't been used since —"

"Rotate teams every ninety seconds." Ethan tossed him a stick of Nobel's blasting gelatin. "Collapse the eastern approach. Clara?"

The cowgirl grinned through bloodied teeth. "Yeah, boss?"

"Can you ride?"

"Try and stop me."

Ethan's nod held more respect than words ever could. "Take the mustang herd through Ghost Canyon. Make noise."

As Clara hobbled toward the corral, Lily pressed a clay jar into her hands. "Open this when the mists come."

***

The Valley's Breath rose as shadows lengthened—not the gentle evening fog of frontier ballads, but a living thing that writhed between cottonwood trees. Langston's advance scouts found themselves shooting at vapor shapes that mocked them with whispers.

"Over here, you bastards!" Clara's voice echoed from a dozen directions as she galloped through the spectral haze, Lily's jar emitting plumes of iridescent pollen. The mustangs' hooves threw sparks from flint deposits hidden beneath topsoil, setting the mist aglow with witchfire radiance.

A New Orleans recruit in Langston's ranks crossed himself. "C'est le Diable!"

By dawn, survivors would swear they'd fought phantoms—trees that grabbed like hands, streams flowing uphill, and the very air resisting their passage. But in that moment, there was only the Valley's ancient wrath made manifest, swallowing greed whole.

***

The Valley's Wrath

Lead sang through the pines as Langston's men pushed harder, their numbers swallowing whole chunks of territory only to lose ground when the valley itself fought back. A mercenary screamed somewhere west, his shinbone snapped by a sudden fissure in what had been flat earth minutes before. Ethan's defenders moved like ghosts through the smoke—here a rifle barked from behind a boulder, there a bowstring thrummed from a ridge already abandoned.

Lily Chen crouched behind a lichen-crusted rock, fingers clawing at roots beneath the soil. Blood dripped from a gash above her eyebrow, blurring her vision as she pressed her jade pendant to the earth. "*Wù zhǎng*," she hissed, the pendant growing warm against her palm. Thistle vines erupted from the ground, barbed tendrils coiling around three advancing miners. One man fired wild, the bullet tearing through Lily's sleeve as she rolled away.

"Persistent *cào dàn*," she spat, scrambling toward a stand of aspen. Her boot snagged on a half-buried skull—some ancient defender, perhaps. The bones crumbled as she kicked free, and for a heartbeat, the air tasted of sage and grief.

Twenty yards downhill, steel rang against steel as Deke O'Sullivan blocked his brother's saber strike with a rusted pickaxe handle. Jasper's grin flashed like a snake's underbelly. "Still fighting with scrap iron, brother? Some tracker you turned out to be."

"Better'n being Langston's bitch," Deke growled. His boot caught Jasper's knee, sending them both sprawling into scree.

Jasper lunged first, fist cracking against Deke's jaw. "You left me swinging in Cheyenne! Three days in that goddamn gibbet!"

Deke headbutted him, tasting copper. "You sold out the McAllister gang!"

"For *us*!" Jasper scrambled backward, hand closing around a jagged stone. "You think honor fills bellies?"

The rock came down. Deke twisted, the blow glancing off his shoulder. They grappled like feral dogs, years of betrayal and stolen chances boiling into elbows and knees.

***

Clara Benson didn't see the hatchet until it was airborne. She tackled Old Tomás into the mud as the blade thunked into a wagon wheel behind them. "Christ on a biscuit! You tryin' to collect arrows with your teeth?"

The old cook blinked up at her, clutching a cast-iron skillet like a talisman. "They're flanking the root cellar!"

Clara squinted through powder smoke. Four of Langston's boys were dragging a nitro crate toward the valley's food stores. Her gut clenched— same move she'd helped plan weeks ago.

"Gimme that." She snatched the skillet, sprinting low along a dry creekbed. Bullets kicked up dirt around her boots as she cleared the rise. "Hey, shitkickers! Supper's served!"

The skillet connected with a mercenary's temple in a satisfying *clang*. He dropped. His companion swung the nitro crate like a battering ram. Clara dove, grabbing the dead man's revolver. Two shots. The crate tumbled into the creekbed.

"Fire in the hole!" someone yelled.

The explosion lifted Clara off her feet. She hit the mud laughing, ears ringing like church bells.

***

Lily's palms bled as she wove through a thicket of young pines, her pendant hot enough now to scorch skin. Five Langston men pursued, their curses blending with the valley's unnatural howl. She skidded into a moon-washed clearing—and smiled.

Má què cài. Sparrow grass.

Her boot crushed the fragile blue stems as she passed, releasing bitter spores. The first mercenary stumbled into the cloud, clawing at his throat. "Fuck's this witchcr—"

The paralysis hit fast. Three men froze mid-stride, eyes bulging as their muscles locked. Lily snatched the fourth man's pistol, pressing the barrel under his chin. "This valley doesn't like strangers."

The shot echoed.

***

Deke had Jasper's face in the mud when the ground shuddered—Clara's nitro gambit, probably. The tremor loosened his grip. Jasper bucked, flipping them over. His thumbs found Deke's windpipe.

"Remember... Da's farm..." Jasper wheezed, blood dripping from his nose. "You... always... choked..."

Black spots danced in Deke's vision. His hand scrabbled blindly, finding Jasper's belt knife. The blade slid between ribs with the ease of shared memories—stolen apples, their mother's laugh, a hanged man twisting in Cheyenne square.

Jasper stiffened. "Ah... *fuck*..."

He collapsed sideways, breath bubbling red. Deke rolled onto all fours, vomiting bile. Somewhere beyond the ringing in his ears, a familiar voice drawled, "Hell of family reunion."

Ethan Blake stood over him, offering a hand streaked with black powder. Behind him, the valley burned in patches—amber flames licking silver-leafed trees, defenders dragging wounded toward Lily's makeshift hospital.

"Not done yet," Deke rasped, accepting the pull up.

"Course not." Ethan tossed him a fresh Colt. "Jasper's boys are rallying near the gorge."

Deke checked the cylinder. Six rounds. Same as the number of siblings he'd buried. "Let's disappoint 'em."

***

Clara limped past them, hauling a water bucket toward the fighters. A Blackfoot archer nodded as she passed—first acknowledgment that wasn't a glare. Her bandana hung in bloody shreds, but the weight she'd carried since betraying these people finally cracked.

"Benson!" Ethan called.

She turned, expecting another suicide mission. Instead, he threw her a nod—the kind given between warriors. No words needed.

The valley's howl rose again, this time carrying the salt-scent of distant rain. Somewhere beyond the smoke, thunder walked on bone-dry hills.

***

The smell of burnt sage and iron hung thick where Aiyana Whitefeather knelt, fingers pressing a poultice against a Blackfoot fighter's gut wound. Her braids had come half-undone, feathers dangling like broken

146

promises. "Breathe shallow," she murmured, tying off the bandage with hands that hadn't stopped shaking since dawn. Across the battlefield, someone screamed curses in three languages.

Ethan spat blood near the smoldering remains of a supply cart. "Deke! Flare count?"

"Three reds left." Deke reloaded with methodical precision, eyes never leaving the tree line. His shirt clung to him like a second skin of sweat and gunpowder. "Langston's boys pulled back past the twin oaks. For now."

Lily Chen stumbled into their makeshift bunker, sleeves charred and jade pendant glowing faintly through her torn collar. "Need two bodies at the north slope." She grabbed a canteen with blackened fingers. "Thistle's taking root in the burn zones. Slows boot treads if we—"

A rifle cracked. Dirt exploded six inches from her boot.

"Christ's sake!" Ethan yanked her down as three more shots peppered the berm. "Sprout later, Doc. Breathe now."

She flashed teeth in something too feral to be a smile. "Tell that to Langston's blasting caps."

Clara Benson limped past dragging a crate of Springfield rounds, her borrowed shirt stained rust-brown. A Blackfoot teenager tossed her a cartridge belt without looking—first gift that hadn't come with a knife's edge. She caught it mid-stride. Progress, frontier-style.

Deke watched her through the smoke. "Think she'll bolt?"

"Today?" Ethan thumbed fresh rounds into his Colt. "Nah. Reckon she's found better folks to disappoint."

Aiyana appeared suddenly between them, pressing cloth-wrapped bundles into their hands. "Chewed yarrow for the shakes. Don't swallow the fibers." Her gaze lingered on Deke's powder-burned palms. "The valley remembers its defenders."

He pocketed the remedy without comment. Sentiment died easier than men out here.

***

Shadows stretched long when the gunfire stuttered into uneasy silence. Across the scorched earth, lanterns bloomed like fireflies in Langston's camp—too many, too bright. Preparation, not retreat.

Lily crouched by the spring, directing survivors to weave poison oak through the breached fences. Her voice had gone hoarse from shouting herbal ratios. "Double the devil's club near the shallows. Splinters buy us time."

Clara dropped beside her, sluicing blood from a scalp wound. "They're bringing up mules. Heard the handlers cursing crates marked 'nitro.'"

"Charming." Lily tossed her a folded wad of moss. "Press that to your head before you faint. I need every shooter vertical."

Aiyana materialized at the water's edge, studying the ripples. "Ghost Walker's Dance comes early tonight." She nodded west where ground mist curled like phantom rivers between the pines. "The valley answers in its way."

Ethan joined them, carbine slung low. "Answers with fog?"

"With memory." She dipped her hand, sending concentric rings across the dark water. "These lands recall each tread. Every drop of spilled blood. Tonight... they walk."

Deke spat. "Poetry won't stop shrapnel."

"Nor will cynicism." Aiyana stood fluidly, beads clicking in her hair. "Prepare fire arrows. The mists favor close work."

Clara snorted. "Because fighting blind worked so well at midday?"

But Lily was already moving toward the armory, shouting for pitch and rags. Ethan watched her go, then chucked Clara a matches tin. "Welcome to defensive tactics, city girl. Light 'em where the fog glows greenish."

She stared at the tin. "That a real thing?"

"Tonight it is."

High above, the first stars burned through gunsmoke haze. Somewhere in the dark, mules brayed under heavy loads. Men cursed. Metal clanged.

Aiyana tilted her face to the emerging constellations. "Three hours till true dark. They'll come with the moon."

Deke checked his revolver's wheel. Full load. "Let 'em."

Along the perimeter, defenders passed bitterroot tea and fresh ammunition. Someone laughed too loud. Someone else retched quietly. Lily's thistle patches crept unseen through topsoil, reaching for the first bootfalls yet to come.

The valley held its breath.

CHAPTER 15

Heart of the Valley

The Valley's Pulse

ETHAN BLAKE HACKED THROUGH a curtain of devil's claw with his bowie knife, thorns snapping like brittle bones. The valley didn't want company. It hissed at them through sawgrass taller than a man, slapped at their legs with poison oak, spat gnats into their eyes. Behind him, Lily Chen ducked under a low-hanging limb, her fingers brushing a cluster of fungus growing in bark fissures—*Ganoderma*, her brain catalogued automatically—before shoving forward. Aiyana Whitefeather moved like water through the undergrowth, her braids whispering secrets to the wind.

"Keep up," Ethan growled, though it wasn't necessary. The women at his back had more grit than half the men he'd ridden with.

Lily adjusted her satchel, the jade pendant bouncing against her collarbone. "If your *directions* are right—"

"They're right." Ethan kicked aside a rotting log crawling with red-backed beetles. The map in his head burned clearer than any paper—the slant of granite outcrops, the bend where the creek fork split like a snake's tongue. "Chamber's just past the sinkhole. Ten minutes."

Aiyana paused, palm flat against a cottonwood trunk. "Less. If we outrun the rain."

Above the canopy, thunder flexed its fists.

They found the sinkhole by smell first—wet limestone and something older, like turned earth from a coffin's lid. Ethan crouched at the rim, squinting at the moss-slick stones below. The drop wasn't sheer, but the rocks wore a greasy sheen. "Here. Climb down slow. Handholds on the west face."

Lily peered over the edge, her nose wrinkling. "Slow's all I've got in these boots." She looped her satchel crosswise, the jade pendant tucked securely under her shirt. The descent was all elbows and curses, boots skidding on shale. Halfway down, Aiyana froze, her moccasin toe hovering over a crevice.

"Don't," she murmured.

The valley held its breath.

Ethan felt it first—a vibration humming through his boot soles, traveling up his spine. The hair on his arms lifted. Lily's pendant grew warm against her skin.

"Move," Ethan barked.

They hit the bottom running.

***

The chamber door wasn't hidden. It *loathed* you.

A slab of sandstone hunched in the cliffside like a rotten tooth, crusted with lichen and the fossilized shells of creatures that hadn't seen sun in millennia. Symbols gouged into the rock pulsed faintly, their edges glowing the sick green of corpse light. Ethan spat dust, rolling his shoulders. "Back."

Lily caught his arm. "Those markings—they're not Pueblo. Not Anasazi either."

"Older," Aiyana said. Her fingertips hovered an inch from the stone. "Not...*people* marks."

Ethan set his boot against the door. The stone groaned, grudging, as he shoved. Muscle corded in his neck. For a heartbeat, nothing—then the scrape of rock on rock, the sour stench of trapped air rushing out.

The chamber exhaled.

***

Inside, the walls bled light.

Not fire, not oil—something in the stone itself. Veins of phosphorescent quartz snaked through the bedrock, etching symbols that squirmed if you stared too long. Ethan's Colt was in his hand before he'd decided to draw. The barrel swept the room—empty. Just dust, and the hum.

"God Almighty," Lily breathed.

She stepped past him, drawn like a compass needle. Her satchel slid off her shoulder, forgotten. The jade pendant swung free now, its carved herbs catching the quartz-light. As her shadow fell across the nearest wall, the symbols flared.

Aiyana gripped her shoulder. "Careful."

"It's *reacting*." Lily's voice trembled—not fear, hunger. The pendant warmed, then burned. She hissed, clutching it, but didn't let go. "Eth— look at the patterns. Fibonacci sequences in the mineral deposits. Fractal branching in these...*glyphs*, or whatever they—"

"English, Doc."

She spun, eyes wild with revelation. "This isn't a tomb. It's a *battery*."

The walls throbbed in time with her words. Deeper in the chamber, something clicked—stone grinding on stone. Aiyana's knife flashed into her hand. "What did you—?"

"Wasn't me!" Lily backed toward Ethan, the pendant now blazing like a struck match. Shadows writhed. The floor trembled.

Ethan grabbed her elbow, yanking her behind him. "You and your goddamn curiosity—"

A sound cut through—not a growl, not a machine. Something between. The walls peeled apart.

Darkness unspooled.

"Run," Aiyana said.

They ran.

***

Lily's fingers blistered against the jade pendant. The carved *lingzhi* mushroom design seared into her palm like a brand as glyphs swam across the chamber walls. "Not just a battery," she breathed, tracking spiraling patterns that defied Euclidean geometry. "A transformer. Step-down voltage through quartz deposits—can you feel the harmonic resonance?"

Ethan spat blood where he'd bitten his tongue running. "Feel like I stuck my head in a beehive." His Colt wavered between three archways revealed by the shifting stones. "Which damn exit?"

The pendant tugged Lily's neck forward. She gripped Aiyana's wrist, pressing their hands against a wall section humming at 60 cycles per second—exactly matching the tremor in her sternum. "Three-phase system," she muttered. "Neutral line here, see how the malachite veins..." Her words died as overlapping shadows resolved into equations older than Confucius.

Aiyana jerked back. "Your eyes—"

"Voltaic cells!" Lily's laughter edged hysterical as bioluminescent moss flared in her peripheral vision. "The whole valley's a circuit board. Groundwater electrolytes, sedimentary layers as capacitors...Grandmother's stories about dragon lines weren't metaphors."

Ethan cocked his hammer. "Great. Let's chat geology *after* escaping the murder tomb."

The pendant flared. Glyphs burned themselves onto Lily's retinas—flora classifications in no language she knew yet understood completely. "Wait." She tore a page from her field journal, charcoal scraping feverish diagrams. "This chamber isn't the source. It's a *fuse box*. Langston's explosives could trigger cascading—"

Stone grated overhead. Aiyana tackled them both as a limestone slab smashed where they'd stood. "Move now. Philosophize later."

***

Deke tested the bowie knife's edge against his thumb. Still sharp enough to shave with. Good. The Schofield's cylinder clicked under practiced fingers—six .45 Long Colts, each cartridge's rim filed for faster fanning. Not that he planned to shoot anyone tonight.

"Demolition derby," he muttered, wrapping dynamite sticks in burlap. Five bundles. Ten if you counted the sulfuric acid vials taped to his ribs. The moon hung low over Sentinel Range, casting enough light to see Langston's sentry fires dotting Silver Creek like infected wounds.

Leather creaked behind him. Deke had the knife pressed to a carotid artery before his conscious mind registered the scent of Bay Rum aftershave.

"Easy, O'Sullivan." Sheriff Hart stood statue-still, star badge catching stray moonlight. "Came to talk, not tussle."

Deke didn't withdraw the blade. "Heard you sold out to railroad money."

"Funny thing about mining towns." Hart's Adam's apple bobbed against cold steel. "Folks see what you let 'em see." He slowly lifted a leather folio stamped with Langston's private rail code. "Man gets lonely playing chess alone."

The knife withdrew. Deke spat. "Checkers player myself."

Hart massaged his neck, laying out reconnaissance sketches showing guard rotations and powder magazine locations. "They've got twelve cases of DuPont red ash in Boxcar Nine. You breathe on that wrong, we'll be picking Langston's teeth out of Canada."

Deke studied the maps through narrowed eyes. "Why sniff around me? Got deputies."

"Deputies polish badges. You?" Hart produced a whiskey flask, took a pull. "Heard about the McCready Gang. How you turned their own nitroglycerin shipment into an open-casket funeral."

Wind whistled through pines. Somewhere, a screech owl cried. Deke finally grunted. "Dynamite's simple. Men ain't."

Hart's smile didn't reach his eyes. "Langston's foreman pays protection to three different tongs. Crew's jumpier than a whore in church." He tapped a circled name on the roster. "Big Mike Donovan. Beats workers who look at him cross-eyed. Got a sister in Helena."

Deke pocketed the documents. "Keep talking."

"Word is he skims copper wire shipments." Hart produced a tintype photo from his vest. "Might find that interesting. Along with these..." Three brass railroad keys clinked onto the stump between them.

The sheriff stood, brushing pine needles from his coat. "Oh, and O'Sullivan? If you light that fuse before moon-set, I'll make sure the blast doesn't take the water tower." He paused. "Kids play there mornings."

Deke waited until Hart's footsteps faded before examining the tintype. Grainy image showed Langston shaking hands with someone familiar— someone supposed to be dead. He fed the photo to his campfire, watching smiling faces curl into ash.

"Sneaky bastard," he admitted to the night. The acid vials chafed his ribs as he shouldered the dynamite pack. Somewhere in the dark, a meadowlark sang. Deke moved toward it, silent as gun smoke.

***

The chamber breathed around them - ancient stone exhaling secrets through cracks veined with luminescent moss. Lily's jade pendant hummed against her collarbone, its vibration syncing with the symbols crawling across damp walls like mercury on glass.

"Patterns match the river's bend," Ethan muttered, fingers hovering over his mother's journal. He flipped to a page smudged with decades-old pencil dust. "See? The same spiral marking she found near the copper deposits."

Aiyana crouched, palm flat against the floor. "Not just metal. The earth's pulse here..." Her braids swayed as she turned toward a seepage crack weeping mineral-rich water. "This chamber's a heart. Pumping life through the valley's veins."

Lightning cracked outside. Through the arched entrance, thunderheads bruised the sky above Sentinel Peaks. The storm's first fat raindrops hissed against heated stone.

"Langston doesn't want silver." Lily pressed her pendant to a wall symbol that shivered under the jade. The chamber groaned, floor vibrating as hidden water channels roared to life beneath their boots. "He's after the current itself. This concentrated energy could power a hundred stamp mills."

Ethan's knuckles whitened on his revolver grip. "Then we plug the artery." His boots scraped across lichen-crusted carvings as he moved to the chamber's western wall. "Aiyana - your people ever collapse tunnels here?"

"Only fools dig holes in a hornet's nest." The healer stood, wiping iron-scented groundwater from her palms. "But there's an old lava tube above the main aquifer. Drop enough rock..."

Another lightning flash silhouetted three figures in the entrance. Young Tomás from the terraces clutched a Springfield nearly his height. "Blake! Langston's boys are forming up by the south gulch. Got a damn cannon."

Ethan's jaw worked. He tossed Tomás his field glasses. "Red rock outcropping at the pass. Can you hit the overhang?"

The boy's grin showed a missing incisor. "Better'n your sorry ass at poker."

"Mind your angles. And Tomás?" Ethan caught the boy's shoulder as he turned. "Wait for my signal."

The thunder found its echo fifteen miles west, where Victor Langston's boot cracked through a whiskey crate. "You're telling me children are picketing my equipment?" Spittle glistened on his waxed mustache. "I pay mercenaries, not wet nurses!"

His foreman recoiled from the shattered crate. "Sir, the terrain's...unnatural. Mules go lame crossing certain ridges. Men report vertigo near the eastern bluffs."

Langston's signet ring gouged the map table. "Burn the vertigo. Burn the bluffs. Burn every stinking sagebrush until this valley coughs up its riches!" He spun toward the tent flap where a hulking silhouette waited. "Donovan. Take six men. The Greek fire canisters."

Outside, rain sizzled against tarred canvas. Big Mike Donovan's sausage fingers flexed around a cleaver's handle. "What about civilians?"

The industrialist's smile peeled back from gold-capped molars. "No witnesses. No prisoners." A pearl-handled Colt appeared in his hand like magic. "Except Miss Chen. I'll want her...articulate fingers sorting through whatever scraps remain."

At the valley's northern rim, Lily knelt in mud that squelched prophecies between her toes. Her sketchbook lay open to pages crosshatched with root systems and chemical equations. "Here," she barked at two teens hauling woven baskets. "Scatter the nightshade berries along the game trail. Crush the leaves but don't inhale the dust."

Aiyana materialized from the downpour, her beaded cloak shedding water like duck feathers. She studied Lily's diagram - an intricate maze of toxic flora and controlled burn zones. "The thornapple grows thick near the hot springs. Boils the blood if ingested."

"Perfect." Lily's pencil flew across the page. "Can your people guide Langston's scouts that direction?"

"Old Elk's already singing death songs for their horses." The healer turned as Ethan's shout cut through the storm.

He stood atop a granite outcrop, coordinating teams with sharp hand signals. Miners from Silver Creek passed dynamite crates hand-to-hand like sacrament. Blackfoot warriors honed obsidian blades with methodical sweeps of whetstones.

"Blake!" A barrel-chested drifter named Coombs waved a rusted cavalry saber. "Where d'ya want the caltrops?"

"Tree line past the switchback!" Ethan jumped down, boots sinking in slurry. He caught Lily's elbow, voice dropping. "The chamber's heart. If we need to stop the flow..."

She pressed a small vial into his palm. Liquid mercury swirled inside, captured from the sacred spring's edge. "Seed the main fissure with this. It'll destabilize the magnetic field long enough to..." Her words died as distant thunder resolved into cannon fire.

South gulch erupted in flame and screams. The cannonball's arc chewed through pines, splintering trunks into wooden shrapnel. Through the smoke, shadows advanced - twenty? Thirty? Shapes distorted by sheets of freezing rain.

Ethan jammed his hat lower. "Time to see if Blake luck holds." His revolver clicked as he spun the cylinder. Somewhere in the maelstrom, a meadowlark trilled twice. Then the night tore open.

***

The last embers of false dawn bled through smoke-choked pines as Ethan spat blood into the mud. Somewhere downslope, a mule whimpered.

"Fuses set?" He didn't turn from scanning the treeline where shadows rippled like faulty glass.

Coombs' voice came tight as a tripwire. "Enough boom under that ridge to send Langston's grandma to Jesus." The drifter thumbed fresh rounds into his Colt, brass clicking like prayer beads. "Your Chinagirl sure about them weeds?"

Ethan's knuckle brushed the mercury vial in his pocket. "You smell jasmine in a slaughterhouse storm?"

They both sniffed the metallic air - beneath cordite and wet wool hung the faintest sweetness. Coombs crossed himself with a bourbon flask.

Across the barricades, Lily crouched in runoff that steamed where it touched stone. Her jade pendant threw green knives of light across silver maple saplings pushing through frozen earth. "Grow you bastards," she hissed, smearing paste from a buffalo bladder across tender shoots. The plants quivered, thorns swelling to fishhook proportions.

Aiyana's war club tapped her boot. "Your grandfather's formula?"

"Great-great-uncle Chen's rat deterrent." Lily jerked her chin toward the Blackfoot women stringing sinew nets between lodgepoles. "Tell your girls not to touch the red berries after the rain."

Thunder cannonaded from the east. Not thunder - hooves.

Ethan vaulted onto a shattered wagon tongue. "Positions! Remember the play!" Rifles cocked in ragged unison. A Blackfoot teenager vomited quietly behind a water barrel.

Aiyana materialized at Ethan's elbow, her breath frosting the words: "Ghost Walker comes."

The ground mist coiled suddenly, forming phantom bison that stampeded westward. Every native fighter dropped prone. Coombs stared until Ethan yanked him down. "Eyes shut or lose 'em!"

The spectral herd passed through timber like whiskey through bad decisions. Screams erupted from the woods - Langston's scouts caught mid-advance. Horses went insane, flinging riders into waiting brambles. One man's shrill terror cut off as Lily's enhanced maples embraced him with creaking efficiency.

"Now!" Ethan roared.

The valley exploded in overlapping chaos. Dynamite chains lit by flaming arrows. Tripwires spooling barbed confusion. And through the bedlam, three figures moved like blades:

Ethan methodically reloading as he advanced, each shot punctuating tactical commands.

Lily scattering seeds that bloomed into choking vines wherever boots hit soil.

Aiyana spinning through battle smoke, her club cracking knees with the precision of a geologist's hammer.

They met at the shattered remains of the old trapper's cabin. Lily tossed Ethan a fungus-studded pinecone. "Breakfast?"

He bit hard, wincing at the bitter rush of alertness. "Tastes like your mother's perfume."

"Same active ingredient." She adjusted his grip on a stolen cavalry saber. "Don't stab downward - the poison splashes."

Aiyana watched Langston's forces regroup on the scree slope. "Second wave brings the cannons."

Ethan spat brown saliva. "Let's invite them closer."

Coombs appeared with a whiskey keg full of nails and desperation. "Darlin', light this when I croak."

Lily tied the fuse with surgeon's knots. "You'll outlive regret."

As dawn's first truth breached the mountains, the defenders raised a sound no army could replicate - Blackfoot death chants harmonizing with Chinese work songs, miners' curses weaving through both. Ethan met Lily's glance, then Aiyana's. No nods. No speeches. Just three sets of teeth bared in identical grins.

The rocks began to bleed Langston's men.

CHAPTER 16

Nature's Judgment

*T*HE AIR TASTED LIKE *gunpowder and bad decisions.* Ethan Blake spat blood into the dirt, the crack of rifle fire shredding the morning quiet. He crouched behind a lichen-crusted boulder, fingers checking the cylinder of his Colt. Six shots left. Forty invaders scrambling up the scree slope below. *Plenty to go around.*

"Flank right!" Ethan barkedt at the trio of leather-skinned ranchers hunkered nearby. "Draw their fire while Chen's boys hit the gully." The men moved like sagebrush ghosts, decades of hunting mountain lions making them disappear into the rocks. Exactly how Pa would've done it. Exactly how Deke taught them last week.

Lily Chen's voice cut through the chaos from somewhere above. "Ethan! Twelve o'clock - *wǎnyī* grass!" Her jade pendant flashed emerald through the haze as she pressed both palms against a lightning-struck ponderosa. The tree shuddered, releasing a cloud of iridescent pollen that made three charging gunmen start sneezing uncontrollably. One shot his own boot clean off.

"Appreciate the assist, Doc!" Ethan lobbed a stick of dynamite into a cluster of Langston's men trying to scale the cliff face. The explosion sent bodies tumbling like rag dolls. "You growing carnivorous weeds yet?"

"Working on it!" A thicket of wild rose suddenly erupted through a weapons crate, vines snapping rifle stocks like kindling. Lily didn't look up from whispering to a knot of twisted juniper roots. "Need me to grow you a sense of humor next?"

The ground started trembling before the sound hit - a low thunder rolling from the eastern ridge. Deke O'Sullivan's bay mare crested the rise first, teeth bared like she wanted blood instead of oats. Twenty riders fanned out behind him, stolen Langston Mining Co. bandanas tied around their faces.

"Y'all ready to eat some goddamn *dust?*" Deke roared, spurring his mount downhill. The posse hit Langston's flank like a sledgehammer to ribs, scattering mercenaries beneath steel-shod hooves. A kid barely old enough to shave took a shotgun blast to the chest mid-charge. Deke didn't break stride, putting two rounds through the shooter's forehead as he rode past.

Victor Langston's silver flask hit the mud. "God *damn* these backwater idiots," he hissed, watching his advance teams collapse through brass field glasses. His tailor-made suit was splattered with somebody else's brain matter. "Burn the western tree line! Flush them into the open!"

A weasel-faced lieutenant paled. "But sir, the fire could-"

Langston's derringer appeared pressed against the man's carotid. "You smell smoke, son? I do." His smile showed too many teeth. "Let's see how brave these dirt-farmers are when their precious forest becomes hell's waiting room."

Ethan smelled the kerosene before he saw the flames. "Shit. They're torching the aspens." He vaulted over a burning log, collar singed where a bullet had grazed past. Somewhere behind the smoke curtain, Lily was coughing violently. "Chen! You alive back there?"

"Barely!" She emerged dragging a pine sapling by its roots, face smeared with soot. The little tree's needles were vibrating like plucked guitar strings. "Groundwater's shifting. There's a sinkhole under their artillery wagons."

Deke materialized beside them, blood dripping from a split knuckle. "How precise you need this?"

"Fifteen yards due east." Lily tossed him a pebble glowing faintly green. "Drop this where you want the earth to open up."

The outlaw caught it mid-stride, already swinging back onto his horse. "Be back 'fore this rock stops warm." His charge took him straight through a hail of buckshot, coat tails flapping like battle flags.

Langston's artillery captain never saw the glowing pebble roll under his ammunition crate. The ground yawned hungry beneath six tons of cannons and gunpowder. Deke's laughter echoed across the battlefield as the entire eastern flank disappeared into a cloud of dirt and screams.

"Beautiful work, Mr. O'Sullivan!" Lily called out, already redirecting willow branches to snuff the advancing fires. "Ever consider botany as a profession?"

"Rather swallow my boots," Deke growled, but Ethan caught the grudging respect in his eyes.

Victor Langston's fist shattered the lens of his field glasses. "Enough!" He kicked the nearest mercenary toward the carnage. "All units push north! I want that valley's throat in my hands by noon!"

A grizzled scout grabbed his arm. "Sir, the terrain turns to box canyons up there! It's a deathtrap!"

Langston's knife found the man's spleen before he finished speaking. "First man to the heart of this godforsaken valley gets the deed to San Francisco whorehouse," he shouted, wiping the blade clean on a dead man's shirt. "The rest get to die poor!"

The remaining attackers surged forward like rabid dogs, desperation overriding survival instinct. Ethan sighted down his Winchester at the silver-haired devil rallying troops through the smoke. "There's our mark." The rifle kicked against his shoulder. Langston's hat spun away, revealing a bleeding scalp wound.

"Missed," Deke observed drily, fanning his revolver into the mob.

"Did I?" Ethan nodded to where Langston was stumbling backward, clutching his head. The mercenaries hesitated just long enough for three ranchers to pick off their front runners.

Lily's hand gripped Ethan's elbow, her touch humming with unnatural warmth. "The valley's fighting back," she murmured. Through the clearing smoke, the land itself seemed to ripple - streams changing course to flood enemy positions, wind hurling snapped pine needles like shrapnel.

Deke spat a wad of tobacco onto a corpse's face. "About time that lazy bitch pitched in."

***

The rifle reports sounded like popcorn kernels bursting in a cast iron skillet. Ethan spat blood and cordite residue, watching Langston's remaining forces regroup behind a makeshift barricade of dead horses. "They're bunching up near the dry wash," he shouted over the gunfire. Lily knelt beside him, fingers buried in the red clay soil like she was taking the valley's pulse.

"Groundwater's shifting." Her jade pendant glowed moss-green against sweat-damp skin. "There's something..."

The earth bucked like a spooked mustang. Four hundred pounds of pissed-off ponderosa root erupted between attacking mercenaries, spraying dirt and bone fragments. A whiskeyjack screamed past Ethan's ear – except it wasn't a bird. The pine needles swirling around Lily's outstretched hand moved with malicious precision, embedding themselves in eyeballs and gun barrels.

"Christ on a crutch," Deke muttered, emptying his Colt into a fleeing Pinkerton. "Shoulda brought flowers instead of bullets."

The tremor nearly knocked Jasper off his stolen horse. Deke recognized the drunken sway of his brother's shoulders before he saw the scarred face. Same damn posture from when they'd boosted their first stagecoach together – right before Jasper took the whip marks meant for Deke's back.

"Still picking losing sides, little brother?" Jasper's Remington wavered between Deke's chest and a rattlesnake making its escape. "That righteous streak's gonna-"

Deke shot the snake. Then Jasper's reins. The horse bolted, leaving his brother scrambling in the dirt. "You used to know when to fold 'em." Deke advanced, boot heels crunching spent cartridges. Blood dripped from a gash above his eye, making the world look rinsed in burgundy.

Jasper laughed wetly, clutching the arrowhead fragment he still carried in his breast pocket. "Remember when Ma said this was good luck?" He lunged.

They hit the ground like feral dogs. No technique, just twelve years of betrayal and borrowed time. Deke's knuckles split against a gold-capped molar. Jasper's thumbs found the old rope burns on Deke's neck. Somewhere north of consciousness, Deke remembered teaching this chokehold to a greenhorn kid who cried after his first knife fight.

The crack of a breaking rib jarred them apart. Lily stood over the tangle of O'Sullivans, hefting a pickaxe handle carved with Chen family harvest symbols. "The hell's wrong with you two?" She kicked Jasper's pistol into a creosote bush. "We've got live ones still shooting!"

Deke rolled onto his knees, tasting copper. Jasper's smirk dissolved as three Harmonious Botanical Society grandmothers descended on him with hemp rope and what looked suspiciously like poison ivy extract. "Traitor!" one cackled, knotting bonds with the vigor of a woman who'd survived the Taiping Rebellion.

"Same to you, ya batty old-" Jasper's insult dissolved into sputters as a poultice muffled his mouth.

Lily hauled Deke upright by his bullet-riddled suspenders. "Your brother?"

"Not anymore." Deke spat a tooth onto Jasper's chest. "Let's see how he likes being somebody's charity case."

Across the maelstrom, Ethan vaulted over a sandstone outcrop, scanning for silver hair amidst the chaos. Langston's bloodstained Stetson lay trampled near the medicine wagon ruins, but the man himself was scrambling up the talus slope toward Sentinel Ridge.

"Son of a..." Ethan broke into a sprint, dodging crossfire. A mercenary lunged from the scrub – Ethan cracked his skull with the Wayfinder's compass, not breaking stride. The cliff loomed ahead, its sheer face buzzing with enraged hornets displaced from their hive.

Langston stood silhouetted against the cyan sky, derringer in one hand and dynamite bundle in the other. "Blake! Enough of this peasant rebellion!" His manic laugh echoed off the canyon walls. "I'll carve your precious valley into railroad ties and whorehouse shingles!"

Ethan's boot slipped on scree. He caught himself inches from a two-hundred foot drop. "You're out of men. Out of time." He edged closer, the abyss yawning at their periphery.

"Out of *patience*." Langston swung the dynamite like a pendulum. "This territory eats idealists. Your mother's bones are probably-"

The insult died in his throat as Ethan tackled him. They grappled across the crumbling ledge, fingers clawing for purchase on limestone sharp as broken teeth. Langston's diamond cufflink scratched furrows in Ethan's cheek. The dynamite rolled toward the edge.

"You want martyrdom?" Langston rasped, kneeing Ethan's gut. "Let's give them a show!"

Ethan's grasping hand closed around the fuse cord as they teetered over oblivion. Somewhere below, Deke's cavalry horn blared the retreat. Lily's voice rose in a Cantonese battle cry. The dynamite stick slipped, fell, and

—

Silence.

Then the valley itself roared.

***

The dynamite's fuse hissed like a cornered rattlesnake as it tumbled into the void. Ethan's grip on Langston's collar slipped as the magnate twisted, their boots scattering gravel over the drop. Somewhere below, the explosive detonated with a wet *thump* that shook loose stones from the cliff face.

"You sentimental fool!" Langston spat, clawing at Ethan's wounded shoulder. "Should've let me burn with your whore mother's-"

Ethan headbutted him mid-sentence. Cartilage crunched. The cliff edge crumbled.

For three heartbeats they hung suspended – tycoon and protector, fingers interlocked like warring tree roots. Langston's polished boots skidded against empty air, his free hand scrabbling for purchase on stone worn smoother than a river rock. Somewhere beneath them, the silver-tipped aspens began to whisper.

"Let... go..." Langston wheezed, blood bubbling from his broken nose. His manicured nails drew crimson crescents on Ethan's wrist. "Your... precious... code..."

The valley's tremor intensified. Ethan's father's voice surfaced through the adrenaline – *A man's measured by what he carries down from the mountain.* Beneath them, Langston's remaining mercenaries gaped upward, rifles forgotten.

Ethan tightened his grip. "Not today, Victor."

Muscles screaming, he hauled the choking magnate onto solid stone. They collapsed in a heap of labored breaths and bleeding knuckles. Langston's derringer skittered over the edge, its ivory handle flashing before disappearing into the mist rising from the valley floor.

Below, a tobacco-chewing mercenary named Crenshaw lowered his Winchester. "Well I'll be a three-titted jackalope. The bastard saved him."

His companion Rourke stared at the dangling rope still tied around his waist – the same rope they'd used to drag mining equipment through Blackfoot burial grounds last winter. "Ain't natural," he muttered, making the sign of the cross with grimy fingers. "Ain't right."

The dissent rippled through Langston's ranks like wind through wheat. A Chinese rail worker dropped his pickaxe, the blade still streaked with clay from undermining the Three Sisters Terraces. Two Pinkerton agents exchanged their first uncertain glance in a decade of shared brutality.

Above them, the sky tore open.

It began as a green ripple behind Stormcrow Peak – the same luminous jade as the pendant burning against Lily's collarbone. Then came the golds and violets, cascading across the firmament like God's own whiskey spill. The Northern Lights didn't belong this far south, didn't move with such liquid purpose. The colors pooled around combatants, painting war-bruised faces in otherworldly hues.

"Spirit wind!" shouted a Blackfoot rider, throwing his hatchet to the earth. The ceremonial blade sank hilt-deep in soil that had rejected plows for generations.

Down in the arroyo where Deke stood over his brother's unconscious form, the spectral lights glinted off Jasper's brass knuckles. "Hell's bells," the younger Travers brother slurred through split lips, "you joined a damn celestial circus?"

Deke spat blood on his sibling's snakeskin boots. "Joined folks who don't stab backs." He turned toward the luminous sky, absently rubbing the old brand on his forearm where the Bar T Ranch iron had seared loyalty into flesh. The colors reflected in eyes that hadn't witnessed wonder since childhood.

Lily emerged from the aspen grove, her braids crackling with static. The jade pendant at her throat pulsed in time with the aurora's rhythm. She pressed a palm to the nearest tree trunk, bark patterns aligning with the scars on her palm. "Told you they'd listen," she murmured to the shivering leaves. "When shown proper respect."

On the cliff's edge, Langston scrambled backward like a gutshot coyote. "Chemical vapors!" he croaked, swatting at the light beams as if they were horseflies. "Copper deposits reacting with-"

Ethan hauled him up by his ruined cravat. "Breathe it in, Victor." He thrust the magnate's face toward the shimmering expanse. "That's your quarterly reports burning."

The colors intensified. Gold filaments wove between combatants, severing rifle straps and loosening sword knots without cutting flesh. A harmonica's mournful note drifted from the Crossroads Trading Post ruins, though no living lips touched the instrument.

Rourke fell to his knees, clutching a locket containing his sister's likeness – the same sister lost to a Philadelphia poorhouse fire. "We're... we're trespassing something fierce, ain't we boys?"

Crenshaw's chaw-stained spit landed near Langston's Italian loafers. "Pay's good. Ain't *this* good." He slung his rifle across his back with trembling hands.

The surrender spread faster than prairie fire. Mercenaries placed weapons in growing piles that soon resembled steel harvest mounds. Aiyana Whitefeather emerged from the medicine grove, her healing satchel glowing with the same unearthlight as the sky. Without a word, she began tending enemy wounds, her beads clicking a rebuke with each step.

Langston made a final lurch toward the dynamite crate. Ethan's boot came down hard on his wrist. "Your men are leaving," he said, nodding to the exodus forming along Spirit Creek. "Your funds are frozen. Your name?" He gestured to where the aurora's embrace was erasing the LANGSTON MINING CO. brand from supply crates. "The valley's rewriting the deed."

The magnate's laugh sounded suspiciously like a sob. "This isn't over, Blake. There are other valleys. Other fools."

"Sure." Ethan scooped up a fallen revolver, spun the chamber, and handed it to his enemy butt-first. "But you'll need this more than me where you're headed."

Below them, the surrendered mercenaries broke into spontaneous applause as a pair of rustlers freed their last stolen mustang. The Valley's

Breath shimmered across tear-streaked faces, gunpowder residue, and the first honest smiles some mouths had worn in years. Somewhere in the luminous haze, a Blackfoot elder began chanting the same blessing once given to Lewis and Clark – and withheld from every opportunist since.

Lily appeared at Ethan's side, her fingers brushing the fresh scratches on his neck. "Chen would've charged two tonics for that patching job."

Ethan watched Langston stumble downhill toward his departing men – men who now stepped aside rather than aid their former master. "Put it on my tab."

Overhead, the aurora burned itself into every retinas present. It would linger in dreams and drunken tales for decades – the night Montana's wild heart finally broke its would-be breakers.

***

The valley smelled like burnt sage and redemption. Ethan spat blood onto shale that glittered with spent cartridges, his ribs screaming every time Deke thumped his back hard enough to dislodge battlefield grit.

"Next time," the Irishman growled, "maybe *don't* play nice with the bastard aiming to fill your skull with lead." His beard still smoked where a bullet had grazed his cheekbone.

Lily materialized through the haze, fingers already probing the gash on Ethan's forearm. "You'll need yarrow poultice. And whisky." Her jade pendant swung dangerously close to his wound. "The drinking kind, not the disinfecting."

"Both," Deke suggested, tossing a dented flask to a Blackfoot boy darting between the wounded. Across the terraces, former rustlers and elders hauled splintered timber for makeshift stretchers, their movements syncopated with Aiyana's low chants.

Ethan watched a reformed cattle thief press his bandanna to a mercenary's gut wound. "Didn't figure you for a human salvage operation, O'Sullivan."

The outlaw-turned-commander shrugged, reloading his Mare's Leg with grease-blackened hands. "Valley sorts its own." His eyes tracked Jasper slinking toward the tree line, hands raised in permanent surrender. "Mostly."

Aiyana's voice cut through the clamor like an eagle's cry. "The Flowing Fields drink today's blood." She knelt, pressing palms to churned earth where strange green shoots already pierced the mud. "Tomorrow's roots grow deeper."

Lily tied off Ethan's bandage with a sharp yank. "Chen family remedy. Guaranteed to prevent infection and..." She paused as thunder rumbled from cloudless skies. "...irritate the patient thoroughly."

The surviving defenders coalesced around the shattered mining equipment - Chinese laborers teaching Blackfoot warriors how to repurpose drills into irrigation tools, weathered prospectors swapping Colt Peacemakers for pickaxes. Someone produced a battered harmonica and a verse of "Sweet Betsy From Pike" that immediately devolved into a Sichuan mountain ballad.

Deke snorted at the discordant symphony. "Christ. We nearly die for this racket?"

Ethan scooped up a twisted length of silver pipe, its metal still warm from the fight. "Better than Langston's ledger books." He tossed it onto a growing pile of scrap destined for the living terraces' repair.

As moonlight filtered through lingering auroral tendrils, the valley exhaled. Ghost Walker mists curled around bullet-splintered pines, weaving silver through blackened branches. Somewhere in the healing dark, a child laughed.

Lily's shoulder brushed Ethan's - once, twice. No third time needed. Together they faced the wounded horizon, breathing in gunpowder and renewal, while below them the Two Paths economy bartered bullets for seed corn and called it progress.

CHAPTER 17

Healing the Land

LILY CHEN'S FINGERS DUG into the cold mud like surgical instruments, black soil caked under nails that hadn't seen a proper scrub in weeks. "Not dead," she muttered to the crushed yarrow stem, thumb brushing over fractured leaves oozing bitter sap. The jade pendant burned against her sternum—not fire-hot, more like holding a live coal in your mouth without getting scorched.

"Stupid bastards didn't even notice you," she told the plant, peeling back trampled topsoil to expose hair-thin roots. Her grandmother's voice chided in memory—*Xiǎohuā, medicine grows where respect lives*—as she mixed charcoal from last night's cookfire into the dirt. The pendant's glow intensified when she pressed salvaged comfrey poultices against broken stems, light pulsing in time with her heartbeat.

Across the valley, Ethan Blake let the shouting match bounce off him like hail off a tin roof. Two dozen pissed-off souls crammed into the old assay office, sweat and woodsmoke clotting the air.

"Your people shoot first and ask shovel questions later!" A prospector's knuckles whitened around his dented canteen, gesturing at the hidden society elder across the splintered table. "How's my crew supposed to—"

"Your *crew*," the elder interrupted, voice like rusted hinges, "dug trenches through sacred ground."

Ethan stepped into the argument's path before it could draw blood. "Mackenzie." He locked eyes with the prospector. "You needed clean water for your sluice boxes." Pivot to the elder. "Atahensic. They didn't know the burial mounds existed." His boot nudged a warped floorboard. "Both sides lost people to Langston's idiocy. You want to keep losing them?"

The room held its breath.

"Compromise," Ethan continued, pulling a folded map from his jacket. Finger traced a creek's jagged contour. "Redirect the runoff here. Your crews get water." Nodded to the elder. "We mark the graves properly. Burn tobacco, say the words."

Silence stretched taut.

Mackenzie spat brown juice on the floor. "Goddamn hassle."

Atahensic's bone necklace rattled as she leaned forward. "Your machines stay west of the red oaks."

"Deal." Ethan slapped the map down before either side could reconsider. The pendant's distant glow flickered through cracked window glass like a approval rating his choices.

Deke O'Sullivan kicked a saddlebag full of rusty nails toward the ex-mercenaries. "Congratulations, princesses. You just enlisted in the world's shittiest quilting bee."

The men stared at the collapsed barn skeleton like it'd asked them to recite poetry. One giant with a broken nose picked up a warped plank. "What's this for?"

"Making less work for me." Deke yanked a hand-forged saw from his belt. "Three teams. Team one strips usable lumber. Team two digs new foundation trenches. Team three gets to explain why their mothers didn't raise complete morons when the walls collapse."

Chuckles rippled through the group. The giant grinned. "Which team you on, boss?"

"I'm the pretty face motivating you dipshits." Deke tossed the saw— handle first—to a twitchy kid clutching a bandaged arm. "Start slow.

Blade's sharper than your life choices."

Victor Langston found Ethan by the whiskey stash—half-buried crates under a tarp that reeked of desperation and poor decisions. The tycoon's silk waistcoat sported actual dirt stains now. Progress.

"Blake." Victor's polished drawl cracked like dry leather. "Need a word."

Ethan didn't look up from inventory lists. "Talk faster than my bullet."

"Twenty thousand dollars." Victor's throat bobbed. "In a Denver bank. For rebuilding efforts."

The pencil stilled. "Conditions?"

"None." Calloused palms faced outward—a banker's surrender. "Well. One." He nodded toward Lily kneeling in distant mud, green light swirling around her like drunken fireflies. "Let me fund her research. Proper equipment. Supplies."

Ethan finally met his gaze. "Why?"

"Because..." Victor's jaw worked, chewing through pride like gristle. "Ruth made me promise. Before the fever took her."

The admission hung between them—raw and improbable as a diamond in a shit heap. Ethan studied the numbers again. "You screw this up..."

"I'll be the first corpse feeding those yarrow plants." Victor extended a hand that didn't quite tremble. "On my daughter's grave."

Ethan spat in his palm before shaking. "Welcome to the quilt-making party, Mr. Langston."

Somewhere west, Deke's saw started rasping through pine knots. The rhythm almost sounded like hope.

**

The hammer came down crooked, bending a nail that screamed like a stepped-on cat. James Blake caught his son's wrist before the second swing. "Hang that on the barn door, they'll think we're building a torture chamber."

Ethan shook him off, heat crawling up his neck. "I'm aware how to drive a damn nail."

"Course you are." James thumbed the warped metal free. "Just figured after three years avoiding my letters, you'd aim better." Across the scorched barn frame, two whiskey bottles stood sentry on a sawhorse—one half-empty, one untouched since morning.

Clara Benson's voice carried from the south pasture, sharp as a spur jab. "No, *dào gē* means cut *toward* the grain, Mr. O'Hara! You're hacking like a drunk nun at confession!" A chorus of mismatched laughter followed.

James nodded toward the sound. "That firebrand teachin' Chinese plow techniques to Irish railmen?"

"Swedish." Ethan selected a fresh nail. "Oskar's from Malmö."

"Christ." James spit on his palms, gripping the beam they were patching. "Place needs a damn phrasebook more'n lumber."

The silence that followed tasted like rust and pine pitch. Ethan focused on the rhythm—strike, sink, strike—until his father's voice cracked like dry kindling.

"Sarah wanted me to stay."

The hammer hovered. Below them, the Three Sisters Terraces sprawled golden in the fading light, corn leaves whispering secrets to the barley.

"When the railroad offered chief surveyor..." James traced a knot hole shaped like Montana. "She said chasing progress would burn both ends clean off me." He nodded at Ethan's vest pocket where Sarah Blake's journals pressed against his heart. "Smart woman, your ma."

Ethan drove the nail home. "Left her raising two kids alone."

"A lifetime ago."

"Funny." Ethan's knuckles whitened around the hammer. "Still feels like yesterday watching her bury Rachel."

James flinched like he'd taken buckshot. Beyond the barn, Deke's crew started hollering as their salvaged waterwheel creaked to life, its copper veins glinting through the sawdust haze.

"Your sister..." James reached for the untouched bottle. "Never told you this, but—"

"Save it." Ethan snatched the whiskey first. "You don't get to rewrite history because Langston's check cleared."

A shadow fell across the warped floorboards—Lily Chen with armfuls of yarrow stalks, her jade pendant casting leaf patterns on the walls. "Blake? We need you at the treaty table. Granny Wen's threatening to poison the coffee if negotiations take longer than dumpling steam."

James raised a brow. "That the fancy botanist or your parole officer?"

"Both." Ethan stood, back popping like a Winchester cartridge. "Stay out of the liquor."

"Wouldn't dream of it," James lied smoothly, eyeing the bottle with the hunger of a man three days into sobriety.

***

Clara's boot connected with the storage crate. "Sweet bleeding Judas, who packed the seed grain next to blasting powder?"

Fifteen faces stared—Blackfoot elders squinting at Swedish miners, Chinese herbalists elbowing Cornish engineers. All united in bafflement at the redheaded whirlwind rearranging their disaster of a supply depot.

"This..." She jabbed a shovel at the offending crates. "Is dumber than teaching geese tap shoes. Feng shui ain't just for tea gardens, people!"

An Irish voice piped up. "The hell's feng shui?"

"Means stop being an idiot sandwich!" Clara vaulted onto a barrel, braid whipping like a mustang's tail. "Listen up—medicines go west wall, dry goods north, tools east. Who here can't read Mandarin symbols?"

Six hands rose.

"Perfect." She tossed bundles of red-tagged rope. "Tie these around anything that goes boom. Green tags for food, yellow for..." Her nose wrinkled at a crate's contents. "Are those *human teeth*?"

Chester Milburn doffed his cap. "For the bone orchard, ma'am. Proper calcium mulch, see?"

"Christ on a cracker." Clara pinched the bridge of her nose. "New rule —no body parts without labels. Now!" She clapped sharply. "Let's move like we've got sense instead of pudding between our ears!"

As the crew scrambled, a Blackfoot grandmother chuckled deep in her throat. "Little storm cloud," she told Clara in halting English. "Good chaos."

"Learned from the best." Clara winked, tossing the elder a licorice root from her pocket. "Keep this handy for when O'Hara starts crying about calluses."

***

Lily Chen knelt in the shadow of Sentinel Peak, her fingers mapping the land's pulse through a tangle of bloodroot stems. The jade pendant against her collarbone thrummed like a hummingbird's heart, its light mingling with the Valley's Breath swirling overhead.

"See the pattern?" She guided young Mei-Ling's hand along the plant's veins. "Angled growth means mercury's leaching from Langston's old mines."

The girl frowned. "Can we fix it?"

"Maybe." Lily pressed a petal to her tongue—bitter with a metallic aftertaste. "Your grandfather's terraces... Do they still use the ironweed buffer?"

Mei-Ling nodded, black braids bobbing. "Gong Gong says the stones sing when the fog comes."

A sudden breeze parted the shimmering air above them, revealing the ghostly silhouette of the Living Terraces etched into distant cliffs. Lily's pendant flared green-gold.

"Wind's changing." She stood abruptly, clay clods falling from her skirt. "Tell the council we'll need twelve copper basins and every scrap of sphagnum moss within ten miles."

"But the treaty signing—"

"Will mean jack if the aquifers collapse by solstice." Lily was already moving, mind churning through variables. She paused mid-stride as the Valley's Breath curled around her wrist like an affectionate serpent.

Mei-Ling gasped. "It likes you!"

"Let's hope so." Lily pressed her palm to the earth, feeling the telltale vibration of underground streams going sour. "Because we're about to rebuild an ecosystem from the guts up."

***

Ethan faced the bargaining table—an actual door laid across cider barrels —where Granny Wen's bone-handled knife pinned down a map stained with tea and suspicion.

"Our terms stand." The old woman tapped the blade near Silver Creek. "No wheels deeper than Willow Bend. No fires after sundown."

Across the makeshift table, a Cornish engineer bristled. "And where exactly are we supposed to piss, your highness? The moon?"

Before Ethan could speak, a Swedish voice interjected. "Latrine trenches worked in Malmö mines. Forty men, zero cholera."

Granny Wen's eyes narrowed. "You stable animals in Malmö?"

"Better." Oskar grinned, missing three teeth. "We drink."

Ethan massaged his temple. "Compromise. Latrines dug fifty paces past the bend, lined with lime and charcoal." He glanced at the notes from his mother's journal lying open to a page titled 'Sanitation vs. Sanctity'. "Guarded by rotating shifts from both factions."

Silence thickened like gruel. A Blackfoot elder spoke next, his words translated by a teenager with an Edison bulb necklace. "The river spirits demand payment for disturbance."

Langston's banker nearly choked on his cigar. "Payment? We're funding your entire—"

"Two hundred willow saplings," Ethan cut in. "Planted along the banks by equinox." He met the elder's gaze. "Roots to filter runoff, branches for basket weaving."

The translator hesitated. "He says... whose hands will plant?"

Ethan didn't blink. "Mine. And yours. And his." He pointed around the circle—miners, healers, track layers, elders. "Every soul who drinks this valley's water."

Granny Wen yanked her knife free. "Deal."

As hands began shaking—some reluctantly, others with tears—Lily burst through the flap door reeking of sulfur and triumph. "We've got six hours before the aquifers implode. Who's ready to reroute a river?"

Outside, the Valley's Breath pulsed once in time with the jade pendant's glow. Somewhere beneath their boots, the land exhaled.

***

Deke O'Sullivan, the scarred Irishman crouched in the river shallows, calloused hands guiding a banker's manicured fingers around a willow sapling. "Roots face northwest," Deke grunted, his voice softer than any of Langston's men had ever heard it. "Catch the evening mist rolling off Sentinel Range."

The ex-railway enforcer beside him snapped a root. "Christ's sake, O'Sullivan—it's a damn weed."

Deke's knife appeared at the man's throat before anyone blinked. "This weed'll hold your piss-stained riverbank together." He sheathed the blade, then pressed the mangled sapling into the man's palm. "Try again. Slower."

By sundown, twelve former mercenaries could identify seven edible lichens and build a snare that didn't maim prey. One even laughed at Deke's joke about Mormon whiskey.

Langston's silk cuffs were caked in clay as he hauled stones for the new fish weir. A Blackfoot grandmother tossed him a coiled rope. "Tighter loops," she barked, watching his blistered hands fumble the knot.

"Like this?" Victor rasped, blood streaking the hemp.

She spat. "Less thinking. More feeling."

When the weir held against the spring current, the old woman tossed him a tin of rabbit-fat salve. No words. Just a nod sharper than any contract.

***

The Gathering

Clara Benson climbed onto a whiskey barrel, firelight glinting off the Edison bulb around her neck. "Y'all fought over dirt," she shouted, hoisting a jug of something that reeked of pine tar. "Now drink to shared damn dirt!"

The feast sprawled across the Three Sisters Terraces—venison rubbed with Sichuan pepper, fry bread drizzled in honey from Clara's hives. Granny Wen taught tracksuit-clad miners fan-tan rules using bullet casings. Someone's harmonica wailed a Cheyenne lullaby.

Ethan found Lily by the smoking pit, her jade pendant pulsing softly as she turned skewers of medicinal mushrooms. "Still saving us from poison?" he asked, swiping a charred morel.

"Saving *you*," she corrected. "I like these people."

The Valley's Breath swirled above them—not quite northern lights, not quite fog. Deke materialized beside Clara, dripping river muck. "Your still's on fire."

"Feature, not bug!" Clara crowed, shoving a clay cup into his hands.

***

Edge of the Wild

Ethan's boot nudged a cracked ledger half-buried in sagebrush—some dead man's mining claims. Lily crushed it underfoot, wild garlic sprouts already splitting the leather.

"They'll come back," Ethan said quietly. "Railroads. Speculators."

Lily untied her pendant, pressed it against his palm. The jade flared, mapping ghostly root systems through their skin. "Let them. We'll teach the rocks to bite."

Somewhere below, the harmonica choked into laughter. The Breath surged gold, wrapping around their clasped hands like knotted rope.

CHAPTER 18

Guardians of Eden

T HE WIND CARRIED THE sharp scent of burnt sage across the council clearing. Aiyana Whitefeather's braids swayed like pendulum weights as she stepped forward, bone-carved beads clicking against river stones woven into her belt. "You stand where seven generations of keepers stood," she said, voice slicing through the mountain air cleaner than any blade. "Breathe deep. Let the valley taste your intent."

Ethan's calloused thumb found the worn leather of his mother's journal tucked against his ribs. Behind him, Deke shifted his weight—the subtle scrape of boot leather on granite betraying more nerves than the former outlaw would ever admit aloud. Lily's fingers brushed the jade pendant at her throat, her other hand already absently cataloging the medicinal lichen patterns on the surrounding boulders.

Aiyana lifted a birchbark tray holding four artifacts. "Blake."

Ethan approached, the three-tiered terraces of the Living Steps framing his silhouette. She pressed a compass into his palm—not his mother's wayfinder, but something older. The needle quivered toward the stands of whitebark pine guarding the valley's eastern pass. "True north shifts here," Aiyana warned. "Lead others anyway."

Lily's token came next—a clay vial stoppered with pine resin. "Chen medicine needs valley breath now." The jade pendant glowed faintly as she pocketed the vessel, already calculating alkaloid extraction methods.

Deke stared at the arrowhead placed in his palm—obsidian edge flecked with pyrite. "Last man gave me one of these tried planting it between my ribs," he grunted.

"Different edge." Aiyana's mouth twitched. "Teaches better than stabs."

Clara nearly dropped her woven-grass satchel. "I ain't no elder—"

"You track storm rot in root clusters others miss," Aiyana cut in. "Carry that sight farther."

***

Ethan's knuckles whitened around the saddle horn as his mare picked through scree below the sacred falls. The wayfinder compass burned against his sternum. "Damn fool notion," he muttered, rehearsing arguments for the territorial delegates. *We don't trade watershed rights. Not even for steel plows.*

Deke materialized from the tree line, rifle casually slung. "Langston's boys are sniffing around Silver Creek again. Heard they're offering double wages."

"Let them." Ethan adjusted his cuffs—city clothes chafing. "Valley keeps its own."

"Keep telling yourself that pretty lie." Deke spat tobacco juice perilously close to Ethan's polished boots. "Man straddles two worlds gets split cleaner than kindling."

***

Lily's workspace smelled of crushed valerian root and impatience. Glass vials stolen from railroad infirmaries lined crude pine shelves, each labeled in her precise script. She ground night-blooming sphagnum moss with a mortar stone, the jade pendant casting green light across her notes.

"Still mucking with weeds?" Clara leaned against the doorframe, arms crossed over her patched flannel.

"Anticholinergic properties." Lily didn't look up. "Simon's muscles spasm less if—"

"Save the Latin. Need something for frost blight on the squash vines."

Lily tossed a salve tin. "Rub it on the leaves. And Clara? The *Hepatica nobilis* near the hot springs—don't let the goats trample it."

"Wouldn't dare, Doc." The girl caught the tin mid-air. "Saw your brother coughing blood yesterday."

Mortar stilled. "His lungs heal slower than the rest."

"Or faster. Depending."

The pestle resumed its rhythm—firm, controlled. Like heartbeat. Like footsteps. Like the countdown she refused to acknowledge.

***

The mule train creaked to a halt where the Ghost Walker's Dance swirled knee-deep across the pass. Simon Chen leaned against his saddlebags, face gaunt but eyes burning brighter than the fever that nearly took him last winter. "You!" Lily's mortar slipped from numb fingers, crushing moonwort stems she'd been rationing for months.

Brother's grin carved dimples she hadn't seen since Pa's funeral. "Brought your idiot cactus." He jerked a thumb at the swaying pack animals. "Three crates of Ephedra sinica, wrapped in Mama's wedding silks."

She tackled him hard enough to bruise. Simon's ribs felt like kindling beneath his threadbare shirt. "You rode through Langston's territory alone?"

"Had help." He nodded toward the lead mule where a red-tailed hawk perched eying Clara's jittery mare. "Your valley's been sending guides since Butte." His fingers brushed her jade pendant - green light pulsed through his veins, revealing constellations of scar tissue where the consumption ate deepest.

"Christ on a crutch," Lily breathed.

Simon winked. "Told you mountain air works wonders."

***

Deke spat on his whetstone. "Blade's duller than preacher dick."

Twelve-year-old Tomás froze mid-swing, practice stick trembling over the false-tamarack sapling he'd been ordered to defend. "Sir?"

The ex-outlaw snatched the stick, flipped it backward. "Wood's got memory." He dragged splintered end across deer hide stretched between birches. "Grain runs west-east 'cept in stormbent trees. Feel for weakness."

Fourteen hands watched him gut the dummy with three precise tears following hidden rings.

Marta frowned at her own stick. "But Aiyana says violence breaks harmony."

Deke's knife sank into a cottonwood trunk. "Harmony don't stop bullets." He jerked his chin toward the high pass where Ethan was dickering with suits. "That way lies. You guard, or hang meat."

***

Clara's boot pinned the banker's son's wrist before his pocketknife could carve initials into the whispering pine. "Try that again, Pretty Boy, I'll salt your tongue with wolfsbane."

Her trail group shuffled. City folk reeked of lamp oil and bad decisions.

"But Miss Benson..." The Harvard accent made her molars ache. "It's just a tree."

She kicked loose soil over exposed roots. "This here's a nurse log. Rot feeds saplings. Carve it, rot seeps wrong." Her knifepoint traced the Three Sisters irrigation channel half-buried under ferns. "Valley's got rules. Break 'em, you answer to *her*."

They followed her gaze upward where Lily stood silhouetted against shale cliffs, jade pendant blazing as she directed Simon's mule train down impossible switchbacks.

***

Ethan spread the mineral maps across the treaty table. "Silver Creek's aquifers can't handle another stamp mill."

Mayor Langston's cigar ash missed the parchment by a hair. "Son, that valley's squatting on enough argentite to bankroll California."

Outside the railroad car's grimy windows, ethreal fog fingers curled around trestles - the Ghost Walker's Dance testing boundaries. Ethan's mother's compass warmed against his thigh.

"Your drills collapse the thermal vents..." He tapped the honeycomb pattern etched in invisible iron gall ink. "...you lose more than wildflowers. Whole watershed tilts."

Railroad men exchanged glances. They didn't see the hawks circling. Didn't notice their whiskey glasses sweating westward despite stagnant air.

Ethan stood, rolling Blake family charts tighter than a gunfighter's resolve. "Come back when your surveyors learn which way rivers flow."

Laughter died as he stepped onto the tracks where Lily's medicine hawk now perched on the WESTERN PACIFIC sign. It screamed once - the valley's answer to progress.

Lily's mortar ground counterclockwise against pestle stone - three rotations exactly - releasing tendrils of blue vapor that tasted like lightning and river clay. Her jade pendant swung inches above the mixture, casting chartreuse patterns across bubbling liquid. When the last sprig of ghost sage dissolved, she didn't cheer. Just wiped her brow with a shirtsleeve already stained seven shades of green.

"Jiémei," Simon's reedy voice carried through the research hut's birchwood slats. "Still playing witch doctor?"

She found him leaning against the Three Sisters irrigation channel, pretending not to need the polished juniper cane Aiyana had carved. Lily uncorked the flask. "You first."

Simon sniffed. Made a face like he'd bitten into unripe persimmon. "Smells like cougar piss."

"Tastes worse." She didn't blink. "Three drops under the tongue at dawn and dusk."

His chuckle became a cough he tried to smother. Lily watched his shoulders hitch - counting breaths between spasms. When he straightened, sweat glistened on his upper lip. But his fingers closed over hers, steady as mountain bedrock.

"Xièxiè, Lìlì."

The first dose hit like a rockslide. Simon spent three days retching blood-flecked phlegm into clay bowls, skin gone translucent as rice paper. On the fourth morning, he limped into the terraced fields and started replanting storm-wrecked medicinals.

"Chen boy's crazy," grumbled Old Man Two Moons watching from the corn crib. "Should be resting."

Aiyana sorted yarrow blossoms nearby. "Resting killed my grandfather. Work healed him."

By week's end, half the valley's children were trailing after Simon like ducklings. They learned which mushrooms could kill a man or cure fever depending on preparation. Memorized songs in four languages for remembering moon phases. Started calling him "Shūshu" though none shared his blood.

Deke found them clustered around Simon near the waterfall pool, scribbling pictographs in wet clay.

"Lesson's over," he barked. "Guardian drills at high ridge."

Ten pairs of eyes turned pleading. Simon wiped clay-smudged hands on already ruined trousers. "Perhaps our students might demonstrate proper tracking techniques?"

"With respect, Mister Chen..." Deke's scarred jaw twitched. "...tracking ain't fingerpainting."

"Indeed." Simon's cane traced the story-mud at their feet - rabbit hieroglyphs melting at water's edge. "But all good hunters know when to read the earth's handwriting."

The kids held their breath. Deke's boot nudged a crumbling hare glyph. Snorted. Then jerked his chin toward the pines. "Well? You heard the man. Find where them mule deer crossed yesterday. Wrong answers get latrine duty."

As laughter scattered upslope, Deke lingered. Watched Simon's trembling fingers reshape a washed-out bear track. Something tight in his chest unraveled - the old wariness that used to keep him alive. These days, his Colt stayed buried in a cedar chest beneath three wolf pelts and Aiyana's treaty pipe.

Come evening, Deke walked the perimeter. Not the tight patrols of his outlaw years, but the valley's wider spiral path where fireflies winked like earthbound constellations. His calloused palm brushed silver-leafed aspens singing in twilight breeze. Peace sat strange on him still - a saddle that didn't chafe.

When the summons came at moonrise, they found Clara knee-deep in the council firepit, cursing as she arranged ceremonial stones.

"Saints alive! Who designed this deathtrap?"

Aiyana arched one eyebrow. "Our ancestors preferred challenge to pageantry."

Ethan arrived last, trail dust clinging to his only clean shirt. Lily noted the fresh tear in his sleeve, the way his left thumb kept worrying the Blake family compass in his pocket. Negotiation scars.

They stood where the Ghost Walker's Dance first kissed the valley floor - swirling mists lit gold by Aiyana's torch. One by one, voices cut the humming dark:

"By root and rainfall..." Lily's jade pendant blazed like captured starlight.

"...steady as stone..." Clara's fist thumped chest armor forged from salvaged railway steel.

"...eyes open..." Deke's rasp carried from shadowed pines where he'd instinctively taken watch.

Aiyana's burning branch arced overhead, painting the Sacred Run's petroglyphs in fleeting amber. "The land remembers."

Ethan's turn. He stepped forward empty-handed. Drew breath. From the cliffs above came a hawk's shriek - the same that tore through railroad negotiations. The council fire flared cobalt.

"Guess that's our answer," Clara muttered.

Simon's laugh sparked like flint. "Welcome home, guardians."

Far below, hidden springs chuckled through ancient stone. The valley breathed.

***

The council fire's cobalt flames still flickered behind Ethan's eyelids as he found Lily by the storm-washed pine. Her fingers worked the soil where Ghost Walker's Dance had churned mist into mud, extracting a mangled spectacles frame from the muck.

"Your brother's?" He crouched beside her, Blake compass digging into his thigh through denim.

She snorted. "Third pair this month. Man's got the survival instincts of a concussed ferret." Aiyana's ceremonial paint still streaked her collar, jade pendant smeared with ash where she'd clutched it during vows.

Ethan plucked a crushed goldenrod stem from her hair. "Not what I pictured when you said 'research center.'"

"Neither's that." Lily nodded toward Clara's distant swearing - the guardian was teaching recruits how to brew Blackfoot tea using salvaged railway spikes as weights. A toddler sat cross-legged at her feet, solemnly handing her pinecones.

They walked the Sentinel Range's shadowline where Three Sisters terraces stepped down toward the Crossroads Post. Ethan's thumb found the fresh tear in his sleeve - souvenir from negotiating ore rights with Silver Creek suits. Lily's palm pressed against the fabric.

"Still bleeding?"

"Paper cuts from treaty scrolls hurt worse."

Her laugh tangled with the clang of Deke's trainees practicing with repurposed mining tools. The former outlaw leaned against a ponderosa, sharpening his knife on river stone. His nod to Ethan carried the ease of men who'd stopped counting debts.

Lily paused where Harmonious Botanical plots met the Living Terraces. "Simon wants to crossbreed Chen family lilacs with valley sagebrush."

"Christ preserve us."

"Already started." She pointed to a seedling guarded by chicken wire and what looked suspiciously like pages from Mother's journals. "Says it'll smell like..."

"...home meets frontier meets questionable life choices?"

"Exactly." Her shoulder brushed his - warm, solid, smelling of crushed bergamot and gunpowder.

They reached the Whisperwind overlook as the valley exhaled - irrigation wheels creaking, fusion shelters' hide walls snapping in the wind, children's shouts bouncing off sacred run petroglyphs. Lily's pinky hooked around his.

"Never pictured this," she said.

"Which part? The sentient fog or Clara adopting every orphan in Montana?"

"The staying." Her jade pendant caught dying light as she turned. "The building."

Ethan's compass found its way into her palm, brass still warm from his skin. "You told me roots don't chain."

"Neither do compasses." Her thumb traced Sarah Blake's engraving. "Point is, we choose north now."

Below them, Simon emerged from Aiyana's healing lodge trailing six elders and a goat. The Blackfoot women were laughing at whatever joke he'd mangled in their tongue. Across the valley, railway whistles dueled with ceremonial drums as Crossroads Post lanterns blinked awake.

Lily's lips grazed Ethan's stubble. "Suppose we'll need better metaphors."

"Or worse ones."

The wind shifted - carrying Deke's raspy ballads from the training grounds, the metallic tang of Silver Creek's operations, and beneath it all, the clean scent of snowmelt carving its patient path through ancient stone.

CHAPTER 19

Legacy of the Lost Legion

E THAN AND LILY'S DAUGHTER tore through the meadow like wildfire, bare feet churning up dew-kissed clover. A monarch danced just beyond her fingertips, its wings brushing lupine blossoms that scattered pollen like gold dust. She skidded around a granite boulder, giggling as the butterfly veered toward a stand of ancient pines. The trees groaned softly in the wind, their hanging moss stroking her shoulders like old friends. A fox kits watched from a log, tail flicking. "Almost got you!" she hollered, leaping over a creek where trout darted beneath liquid sapphire. The air tasted of ironroot and possibility.

Ethan stabbed the period onto the page hard enough to puncture the paper. His knuckles ached from twelve hours of scripting cavalry charges and betrayals, but the ledger's spine fell shut with the finality of a tomb door. Through the cabin window, his daughter's laughter tangled with birdsong. He flexed his ink-stained fingers, staring at the manuscript. "Truth's heavier than lies," he muttered to the empty room. The fireplace crackled as he thumbed the edge of a war medal fused to the cover — Marcus Aurelius' profile melted into a Rorschach smear from that night in '68 when cannon fire turned the Legion's vault to slag. Down by the river, Lily's voice called the girl home. Ethan didn't move. Let the kid chase ghosts a little longer.

Deke spat a stream of tobacco at a bullfrog sunning itself on a rock. Missed by inches. The gaggle of kids perched on the split-rail fence erupted. "That's how your granddaddy cleared out bandits in '52," he lied, scratching the scar across his collarbone. A freckled boy leaned too far forward, nearly toppling into the mud. "Careful, tadpole. Ain't fishin' you out if you drown." Their laughter skittered across the pond. He launched into the story proper this time — the ambush at Rattlesnake Gulch, the stolen payroll, the Comanchero with a snake tattoo who'd tried to stab him in the kidneys. "Took three days to bury the bastards," he said, ignoring the way the littlest girl's eyes went saucer-wide. The frog croaked. Deke grinned. "Quiet, you. I ain't done."

Clara jerked her chin at the banker from Chicago sweating through his linen suit. "See that birch grove? We coppice every seventh spring. Trees grow back thicker'n my Aunt Betsy's cornbread." The dozen greenhorns trailing her scribbled notes. One raised a trembling hand. "But wouldn't clear-cutting generate faster—"

"Faster profits?" She kicked a pinecone into the underbrush. A grouse exploded skyward, making the group jump. "Your teeth fall out fast too, don't mean it's smart." Her red bandana clung to her neck like a second skin. She marched them past terraced fields where wild rye rippled silver-green. "We rotate grazing pastures so the soil don't get notions of rebellion. Same as you wouldn't..." Her boot caught on a root. She stumbled, cursed, recovered. "Wouldn't work a mare to death." The banker mopped his brow. Clara smirked. Valley did its own convincing. Always did.

***

Whiterock's Last Stand

Sheriff Sam Hart spat a stream of tobacco juice that hit the dirt an inch from the prospector's scuffed boot. "Y'all deaf? I said the north pass is closed." The four men shifted like pack mules eyeing a rattler, their pickaxes glinting dully in the afternoon glare. Behind them, Whiterock's weathered boardwalks creaked under the weight of curious shopkeepers pretending not to listen.

The lead prospector—a wiry Texan with whiskey-breath and a Colt that hadn't seen oil since Lincoln was president—stepped forward. "Heard tell there's silver veins thicker than a preacher's—"

"Lies." Sam's thumb hooked casually over his belt buckle, two fingers brushing the walnut grip of his Peacemaker. "You want mining claims? Try Bannack. Plenty ghosts there need company."

A pockmarked kid clutching a rusted shovel piped up. "We got rights to prospect public—"

"Public lands," Sam drawled, cutting him off mid-whine. "Sure. But see that?" He jerked his chin toward the distant peaks where storm clouds bruised the horizon. "Ain't public past Mercy Ridge. Blackfoot territory. You boys fixin' to negotiate with war parties?"

The Texan paled beneath his tan. "Well shit, Sheriff, why didn't you just—"

"Temperance!" Old Miz Peabody's shrill call shattered the standoff as her spotted terrier streaked between the men's legs. Sam hid a grin while the dog sent shovels clattering. By the time order was restored, the prospectors were backing toward their sorry mule team, muttering curses that lacked conviction.

Sam watched them retreat, fingers lingering on the notched handle of his revolver—eight grooves for eight bastards who'd tested him since taking office. The newest mark still smelled of gunsmoke.

Twenty miles southeast, a different kind of light played through the valley. Lily Chen knelt by the creek, calloused hands submerged in cool water as she rinsed medicinal yarrow. Her daughter's laughter snapped her head up—sharp as a hawk's cry.

The girl was a wildfire in human form. Seven years old and already scaling the lightning-scarred pine like a squirrel, jade pendant swinging wildly from her neck. For a heart-stopping moment, one bare foot slipped on brittle bark.

"Mei!" Lily barked, leaping up.

The child caught herself, grinning down with leaves tangled in black braids. "Māma, look! I'm taller'n the smokehouse!" The pendant flared emerald as dusk's first rays pierced the forest canopy, casting the girl in ethereal haloes.

Lily's reprimand died unspoken. That glow...she'd seen it only twice before. Once when her mother lay dying in the Napa Valley opium den, the pendant lighting her final confession. Again when Ethan's fever broke during the scarlet winter, its radiance outshining their cabin's lone candle. Now it pulsed gently against her daughter's sun-browned chest—the land itself smiling on the wild creature who chewed pine sap like candy and could name every mushroom in the valley.

"Come down before you break your neck," Lily called, voice softer than intended.

Mei descended with reckless grace, hitting the ground running. "Race you to the hives!"

***

The sun bled gold across the western ridge, gilding the valley in liquid light. Aspens trembled like coin-stacks in a miser's dream. Down in the meadow, Ethan Blake paused mid-stride, ink-stained fingers tightening around the leather-bound journal in his hand. Twenty years of wilderness living couldn't dull the punch of this view—the way shadows stretched long and lazy across the native grasses, the distant spark of the creek catching fire from the dying sun.

Movement flickered at the tree line. Lily emerged breathless from the woodline, Mei giggling ahead of her. Ethan's chest tightened. Even after a decade, the sight of his wife flushed and disheveled—apron askew, hair coming unpinned—hit like a sapling willow whip.

"Your daughter," Lily huffed, swatting at a bee circling her collar, "is part mountain goat."

Ethan caught Mei mid-leap, hoisting her onto his shoulders. "Chen women," he murmured against Lily's temple. "Always leaving men in the dust."

They climbed the burial knoll where wind whispered through bear grass. From this vantage, the valley unfurled like their stolen Roman map —smoke curling from Clara's teaching huts, Deke's new cabin squatting near the old mine shaft, the hive fields shimmering with late-season pollinators.

Mei squirmed down to chase fireflies. Ethan pressed the journal into Lily's palm. "For her. When she's ready."

Lily traced the embossed title—Legion's Legacy: A Chronicle of Shadows and Light. The pages whispered secrets in dialects dead and born anew. Somewhere below, Mei's delighted shrieks echoed as fireflies winked in her cupped hands.

"Still think we're fools?" Lily asked quietly.

Ethan's laugh lines deepened. "Oh, we're absolutely fools. The best kind."

Their linked hands swung briefly—a pendulum suspended between past and future—before releasing to gather their wildling daughter. The jade pendant glowed its benediction as three shadows merged into one, stretching east toward the coming night.

The hillside buzzed with cicadas throwing their final raucous party of the evening. Deke materialized from the scrub pines like a grizzled phantom, his new deerskin boots suspiciously free of scuff marks. "Brought reinforcements," he grunted, jerking his thumb at Clara emerging from the switchbacks with two apprentices hauling a woven basket of blackberry wine.

"Reinforcements against what?" Lily arched an eyebrow, catching the clay jug Deke tossed her way.

"Optimism." The tracker spat a pine needle over the cliff edge. "Heard tell it's contagious round these parts."

Clara hip-checked Deke aside, her calloused hands already uncorking bottles. "Ignore the old badger. He's still sore about losing three straight hands of poker to Mei last night."

Ethan's laugh got tangled in the breeze carrying woodsmoke from the lower terraces. Below them, the Valley's Breath rippled across the barley fields—not quite mist, more like the air itself had decided to shiver. Mei's abandoned butterfly net lay trampled near the cairn stones, its handle twined with wild hops already climbing toward the first stars.

Deke settled against a lichen-crusted boulder, producing a harmonica from his breast pocket. The opening notes of *Cielito Lindo* warred with the bullfrogs tuning up in the marsh. "Kid cheats," he muttered around the mouth harp.

"Taught by the best," Clara shot back, doling out chipped tin cups. Her braids swung heavy with bronze clasps forged from reclaimed mining tools—each geometric pattern mapping different water rights treaties.

The wine tasted like summer thunderstorms and poor decisions. Lily watched Ethan's throat work as he drank, remembering other stolen liquors in darker times. His hand found hers, ink-stained fingers slotting between her soil-caked ones. Across their joined palms, the faint scars from Comanche arrowheads and frostbite formed their own peculiar constellation.

Clara raised her cup toward the shimmering air above the Three Sisters crops. "To the suckers who thought we'd starve by first snowfall."

"To the bastards who aren't here to see it," Deke added, too low for the apprentices catching fireflies downstream.

The Valley's Breath thickened above the medicinal gardens, taking on the faint green hue of Lily's pendant. Mei's laughter spun up the hillside moments before she did—a comet trailing oxalis petals and indignation.

"Uncle Deke! You promised!" The girl skidded to a halt, brandishing a stick swaddled in spiderwebs. "Said you'd show me how to snare a shadowcat!"

Deke's sigh fogged the harmonica. "Aye, and your ma promised I'd die peaceful in bed. Reckon we're both liars."

Ethan nudged the forgotten journal peeking from Lily's satchel. Its pages rustled with pressed flora and coded entries about Roman aqueduct designs adapted for desert arroyos. "Still think we should've included diagrams," he murmured.

"And let every fool with a compass replicate our irrigation grids?" Lily tapped her temple. "Some maps live better here."

Mei wedged herself between her parents, reeking of pond muck and victory. "Pao Lao brought the baby goats up to the high pasture today. One tried eating Mr. O'Sullivan's hair!"

Clara snorted wine through her nose.

"Lesson learned," Deke growled, scrubbing at his scalp. "Damn nannies are savages."

As twilight deepened, the Valley's Breath began its nightly dance— phosphorescent tendrils weaving through the stands of quaking aspen. Lily felt the old familiar ache beneath her breastbone, that visceral pull when the land sang its wordless hymns. Mei's head grew heavy against her shoulder, the girl's breathing syncing with the distant rush of snowmelt through sluice gates.

"They'll come again," Clara said quietly, watching the apprentices place lanterns along the spiraling footpaths. "Not just prospectors. Railroad men. Soldiers maybe."

Ethan thumbed the rim of his empty cup. "Let them. We've buried bigger monsters in these hills."

Deke's harmonica hissed a discordant note. "Got a new story for the nippers down at the trading post. Tale 'bout a valley so stubborn, even the rocks rose up to guard her."

Lily pressed her lips to Mei's sleep-warm hair. Felt the pendant pulse once, gently, like a second heartbeat nestled against her collarbone. Somewhere beyond the sentinel peaks, a train whistle carved its lonely arc through the gathering dark.

"Let them come," she whispered.

And the land breathed its agreement.

Also by Author

Books By Damon Nelson

Online Marketing Blueprint

How to Position Your Business for Success in the New Digital Era
https://www.amazon.com/dp/1494892200

The Lost Workshop of Leonardo Da Vinci

Solving a series of clues, 4 Teenagers discover Da Vinci's Lost Workshop
https://amzn.to/4hK39ze

The Lodge Beyond Time

A Time-Travel Romance in a Montana Hunting Lodge
https://amzn.to/3Q8xf3O

RSSMasher Secrets

Power User strategies for Super Charging RSS feeds
https://www.amazon.com/dp/B01G9MYOQS

Garage Sale Marketing

Learn the Secrets to Making Your Garage Sale a Huge Success
https://www.amazon.com/dp/1495988325

Sun-Kissed Escapes

The Ultimate Guide to Florida's Best Beach Vacation
https://www.amazon.com/dp/B0D7M5KMDH

Wholesome Duets

Nutritious Recipes for Seniors - Small Batch Recipes for 2 People
https://www.amazon.com/dp/B0CW1M5PJY

Globetrotter's Journey

Delicious Street Food Adventures for Two

https://www.amazon.com/dp/B0CXGC1GW6

Mermaids, Monsters & Marine Marvels

A Fun Coloring Book Adventure Beneath the Waves
https://www.amazon.com/dp/B0D42359LD

Wild Coloring Book Series Volume 1 - Wild Reptiles

Slither, Scale, and Splash: Adventures with Nature's Coolest Reptiles
https://www.amazon.com/dp/B0D59YKHCD

Wild Coloring Book Series Volume 2 - Wild Primates

Color the Amazing World of Monkeys, Chimpanzees, and Gorillas!
https://www.amazon.com/dp/B0D591JJX4

Best Video Marketing Tools

VidPenguin's resources will help get your video to page 1 of Google
https://www.amazon.com/dp/B01G9GTGX0

Amazon Author Page

https://Amazon.com/author/damonnelson

About the author - Damon Nelson

L IFE'S GREATEST STORIES COME from the roads we choose to travel and the people we share them with. As an author, my heart belongs to exploring this beautiful country alongside my wife and our perpetually smiling Australian Shepherd, Sydney, who's never met a road trip she didn't love.

Our family adventures have painted a colorful map of memories across America. We've watched dolphins play in Florida's crystal waters at sunset, discovered charming cafes tucked away in Alabama's historic towns, and shared beignets in Louisiana's hidden courtyards. Together, we've marveled at Texas sunsets that set the whole sky on fire and traced the Southwest's red-rock horizons.

Some of our most treasured memories come from our ventures through the heartland. We've stood in awe beneath Montana's endless sky, watched wild horses roam Wyoming's vast plains, and caught our breath at the raw beauty of the Dakotas. In years past, I even experienced some of these landscapes from the back of a motorcycle, but these days, we prefer the comfortable adventure of family road trips and occasional flights to far-off destinations.

When I'm not exploring with my family or writing, I draw from four decades of experience as an entrepreneur, craftsman, and business mentor to add depth to my narratives. Every role I've played - from home remodeler to business consultant - has taught me that the best stories, like the best journeys, are about the connections we make and the moments we share.

There's always another horizon to chase, another tale waiting to be told, and I'm blessed to share these adventures with my family and readers like you.

Table of Contents

1. Echoes of the Past   3

2. A Botanist's Quest   11

3. Paths Converge   18

4. Whispers of the Land   27

5. The Journey Begins   35

6. Shadows of the Past   46

7. Nature's Fury   55

8. Crossroads   70

9. Secrets Unearthed   81

10. The Hidden Valley   92

11. Echoes of Betrayal   104

12. Sins of the Father   115

13. Lines in the Sand   126

14. The Siege   138

15. Heart of the Valley   150

16. Nature's Judgment   161

17. Healing the Land   172

18. Guardians of Eden   182

19. Legacy of the Lost Legion   192

Also by Author   200

About the author - Damon Nelson   204